Gus Tried Hard Not To Think About Mariah.

Walking in and seeing her bending over that baby coop thing with her sweats clinging to her hips and her hair slipping in wisps from under the scarf she'd tied around her head—it had hit him hard.

Ever since he'd left her that morning, the taste of her still on his tongue, he'd done his best to convince himself that she was just one more attractive woman in a world full of attractive women.

But Mariah had that certain something that reached right inside a man and got him so snarled up he lost sight of all common sense.

Tall, Dark and Handsome: Three very different sexy bachelors say "I do!" You met the tall one in last September's MAN OF THE MONTH, *Alex and the Angel*. Now, meet the dark one in *The Beauty, the Beast and the Baby*. Just wait till you meet the handsome one, coming your way soon!

Dear Reader,

Welcome to the wonderful world of Silhouette Desire! This month, look for six scintillating love stories. I know you're going to enjoy them all. First up is *The Beauty, the Beast and the Baby*, a fabulous MAN OF THE MONTH from Dixie Browning. It's also the second book in her TALL, DARK AND HANDSOME miniseries.

The exciting SONS AND LOVERS series also continues with Leanne Banks's *Ridge: The Avenger*. This is Leanne's first Silhouette Desire, but she certainly isn't new to writing romance.

This month, Desire has *Husband: Optional*, the next installment of Marie Ferrarella's THE BABY OF THE MONTH CLUB. Don't worry if you've missed earlier titles in this series, because this book "stands alone." And it's so charming and breezy you're sure to just love it!

The WEDDING BELLES series by Carole Buck is completed with *Zoe and the Best Man*. This series just keeps getting better and better, and Gabriel Flynn is one scrumptious hero.

Next is Kristin James' Desire, *The Last Groom on Earth*, a delicious opposites-attract story written with Kristin's trademark sensuality.

Rounding out the month is an amnesia story (one of my *favorite* story twists), *Just a Memory Away*, by award-winning author Helen R. Myers.

And *next* month, we're beginning CELEBRATION 1000, a very exciting, ultraspecial three-month promotion celebrating the publication of the 1000th Silhouette Desire. During April, May and June, look for books by some of your most beloved writers, including Mary Lynn Baxter, Annette Broadrick, Joan Johnston, Cait London, Ann Major and Diana Palmer, who is actually writing book #1000! These will be months to remember, filled with "keepers."

As always, I wish you the very best,

Lucia Macro
Senior Editor

Please address questions and book requests to:
Silhouette Reader Service
U.S.: 3010 Walden Ave., P.O. Box 1325, Buffalo, NY 14269
Canadian: P.O. Box 609, Fort Erie, Ont. L2A 5X3

Dixie Browning

THE BEAUTY, THE BEAST AND THE BABY

SILHOUETTE *Desire*®
Published by Silhouette Books
America's Publisher of Contemporary Romance

SILHOUETTE BOOKS

ISBN 0-373-05985-X

THE BEAUTY, THE BEAST AND THE BABY

Copyright © 1996 by Dixie Browning

This edition published by arrangement with Harlequin Books S.A.

Printed in U.S.A.

Books by Dixie Browning

Silhouette Desire

Shadow of Yesterday #68
Image of Love #91
The Hawk and the Honey #111
Late Rising Moon #121
Stormwatch #169
The Tender Barbarian #188
Matchmaker's Moon #212
A Bird in the Hand #234
In the Palm of Her Hand #264
A Winter Woman #324
There Once Was a Lover #337
Fate Takes a Holiday #403
Along Came Jones #427
Thin Ice #474
Beginner's Luck #517
Ships in the Night #541
Twice in a Blue Moon #588
Just Say Yes #637
Not a Marrying Man #678
Gus and the Nice Lady #691
Best Man for the Job #720
Hazards of the Heart #780
Kane's Way #801
†*Keegan's Hunt* #820
†*Lucy and the Stone* #853
†*Two Hearts, Slightly Used* #890
Alex and the Angel #949
The Beauty, the Beast and the Baby #985

Silhouette Special Edition

Finders Keepers #50
Reach Out To Cherish #110
Just Deserts #181
Time and Tide #205
By Any Other Name #228
The Security Man #314
Belonging #414

Silhouette Romance

Unreasonable Summer #12
Tumbled Wall #38
Chance Tomorrow #53
Wren of Paradise #73
East of Today #93
Winter Blossom #113
Renegade Player #142
Island on the Hill #164
Logic of the Heart #172
Loving Rescue #191
A Secret Valentine #203
Practical Dreamer #221
Visible Heart #275
Journey to Quiet Waters #292
The Love Thing #305
First Things Last #323
Something for Herself #381
Reluctant Dreamer #460
A Matter of Timing #527
The Homing Instinct #747

Silhouette Books

Silhouette Christmas Stories 1987
"Henry the Ninth"

Spring Fancy 1994
"Grace and the Law"

† Outer Banks
*Tall, Dark and Handsome

DIXIE BROWNING

has written over fifty books for Silhouette since 1980. She is a charter member of the Romance Writers of America and an award-winning author who has toured extensively for Silhouette Books. She also writes historical romances with her sister under the name Bronwyn Williams.

For Sara. You'll know why when you read it.

One

The going was slow. Just south of Marion, the snow changed to sleet. The roads were a disaster, traffic barely moving. Near the South Carolina state line, the sleet turned into rain. Cold, dreary, windshield-fogging rain. Gus swore, switched on the defroster and wondered how long it had been since he'd last dosed himself with aspirin and black coffee.

He wondered if the burning in his gut was a result of too much of both, or merely a remnant of the flu that had laid him out for a solid week. Not that it mattered. What he needed was coffee, laced with enough caffeine to keep him awake and enough sugar to lend him the energy to keep going.

Three strikes was usually enough to knock any man out of the game. For Gus Wydowski, who had a well-earned reputation for being tougher than your average male, it had taken four.

"Lisa, damn your sweet, greedy soul, I hope you're as miserable right now as I am," he muttered, downshifting to pass a tank wagon lumbering south along I-77.

Lisa Crane had been strike one. Tall, gorgeous Lisa, with her midnight hair, her magnolia skin and her mercenary little soul. A confirmed bachelor, Gus had been relieved when he'd first met her to discover that she was no more interested in settling down than he was.

Their affair had lasted more than six months, which was a record for Gus. As a rule, after a few weeks with any woman he began to get that antsy feeling that made him want to move on, but with Lisa...

Not that he'd ever thought he was in love. Hell, at thirty-nine years old, he had long since outgrown all those old adolescent fantasies.

Still, they'd been good together. Especially in bed. So good, in fact, that Gus had actually started thinking in terms of the future. He had even bought her a ring.

As it turned out, Lisa had begun to think about a future, too, only not with Gus. She had her heart set on one day owning a Ferrari sports car. Gus was satisfied with his 4×4 extended cab pickup truck. She liked sushi, salad bars and Streisand. Gus liked barbecue, beer and bluegrass.

Lisa had a weakness for Italian shoes and champagne.

Gus had a weakness for Western boots and anything sweet.

Gus was unabashedly blue-collar. He had calluses on his hands and a few more on his heart. He'd been around the block a time or two—always with the same kind of woman. His biggest failing was that he was invariably attracted to women who were way the hell out of his league. Long-stemmed, elegant beauties. Classy ladies who were gracious enough to overlook the fact that he was tough as mule hide and a hell of a long way from handsome on anybody's road map.

Lisa had caught his attention when her hat had blown off during a garden party being held next door to one of Gus's construction projects. He'd rescued her hat, and they'd gotten along like a house afire right from the first.

About the same time Gus had started thinking in terms of teaming up permanently, Lisa had started playing games. Breaking dates, leaving town without telling him, coming back without letting him know. The sex that had been so good for so long had become less satisfactory, and they'd usually ended up arguing over whose fault it was.

Gus had a temper; he would be the first to admit that. But he tried not to let it get too far out of hand and never with a woman. He'd been taught by a mother, a grandmother, an aunt and a sister that women were to be treated like fine china. And he had always obeyed that rule. Right up to the night when Lisa had told him she had signed a modeling contract and was moving to New York. She was sorry if he was disappointed, but then, they'd never pretended to anything more than a casual relationship.

Casual. Right.

Gus had told her that he was far from disappointed—a lie. That lately he'd been thinking about moving on—another lie. He'd wished her a lot of luck, but he hadn't specified which kind.

And then, with the engagement ring he'd bought still in his pocket, he'd gone on a bender—something he hadn't done in a long time. He'd ended up putting his left fist through a packing crate. That had been strike number two. Number three had come when he'd gone to the emergency room for a stitch job. There he'd been coughed on and sneezed at until he'd eventually come away with seven stitches, a tetanus booster and a bug that had laid him out flat for nearly a week. The ring had been missing when he'd gotten around to looking in his pockets. Then he remembered giving it to one of the older barmaids and telling her to buy herself a pair of good sturdy shoes with arch supports.

Jeez, no wonder he couldn't cut it with the ladies. When push came to shove, he was about as romantic as a migraine headache.

Gus lived alone in the first house he'd ever built—an A-frame near a small mountain town in North Carolina. The house was far from perfect, but he liked it well enough. That is, he'd liked it until he'd been forced to spend a week alone there, sick as a dog, aching in every bone, alternating between chills and fever.

Then had come strike four. The weather. When he'd finally come around, he'd been snowed in right up to his dormers. His truck, which he'd left slewed in the driveway, was buried door-handle deep. The power was out; his house was cold as a tomb; the phone lines were down; and his mobile unit was still out in the truck.

He'd been weak as a kitten. Still was, for that matter. He'd been hungry, too, but what he'd craved even more than a decent meal was sunshine and the sound of another human voice. Not necessarily up close— just close enough to assure himself that he was still among the living. For a man who'd always prided himself on his self-sufficiency, that was pretty damned scary.

So he'd built up his energy by devouring everything in his efficiency kitchen—ice cream, coffee, stale cinnamon buns and Moon Pie marshmallow sandwiches—and then he'd shoveled himself out. Less than an hour after the snowplow had come by, he had locked up and lit out to find himself some sunshine. With his next two building projects still in the permitting stage and miles of environmental red tape yet to be unraveled, he could damn well afford to lie in the sun and bake his bones until he felt halfway human again.

Just north of Columbia a smoky whipped past, siren screaming, lights flashing, throwing up a muddy spray. Gus swore again. He'd been doing a lot of that lately. He made a quick decision to pull off at the next truck stop and eat something. He was getting down into pecan-pie country. Maybe a slab of pie with ice cream and a pint or so of sweet, black coffee would get him over the hump.

Warily, Mariah eyed the gas gauge on her elderly compact car. It had been known to lie. She should have stopped for gas before now, but she'd been hoping to make it home without spending a night on the road. The trouble was, she hadn't gotten away until nearly noon. Everything had taken longer than she'd expected. Meeting with the super for her share of the deposit on the apartment she rented with two other models, closing out her bank account, packing, trying to get her car serviced, only to be told she could have an appointment the middle of next week. . . .

And then she'd had to deal with Vic. He'd been livid, and a livid Vic was not a pretty sight. He'd reminded her of the contract she'd signed and of everything he'd done for her since he'd discovered her. Then he'd told her he'd been planning to use her in the St. Croix shoot.

She happened to know he was lying about that because only two models were scheduled to go, and Kaye and Danielle had been gloating all morning over snagging that particular plum.

"That's life, kiddo," Kaye had said when she'd tackled her about it. Which summed up Kaye's philosophy in a nutshell.

"That's life right back at you, kiddo," Mariah muttered now under her breath. She'd never gotten the hang of fast, sophisticated repartee. Her mind was still running on Muddy Landing time.

Vic had accused her of not taking modeling seriously, and he'd been right. There had always been an element of make-believe in it. Like playing dress-up, only a lot harder. When it came to make-believe, Mariah would rather choose her own role, and modeling just wasn't *her*.

She'd tried that morning to explain about her brother, Basil, and the baby—about how Basil's wife had run off, leaving behind an eight-month-old daughter, and how his new business was teetering on the brink, and how her family had always depended on her.

Not that Vic had cared. Family? What the devil was family? She was scheduled for fittings! She had runway bookings! Sara Mariah Brady, a nobody from a nowhere place in Georgia, was on the verge of becoming the hottest property since Cindy Crawford, and she wanted to walk out on him to take care of a *baby?*

Well, just maybe, Mariah fumed, reaching forward to smear a circle in the condensation on her windshield, just maybe she didn't *want* to be the next Cindy Crawford! Until Vic Chin had discovered her perched on a ladder, reaching for a kerosene lantern on a top shelf in Grover Shatley's Feed, Seed and Hardware Emporium eleven months ago when he'd stopped off in Muddy Landing to ask directions to Sapelo Island, she had never even heard of the woman. She had been perfectly content with her job as assistant manager of the store.

Or, if not precisely content, at least realistic enough to know that it was the best job Muddy Landing had to offer a woman who didn't own a boat, a set of traps or a business that fronted Highway 17.

And Mariah was nothing if not realistic. As the eldest of five, she'd taken over when her father had walked out, leaving behind an ailing, alcoholic wife and a brood of stairstep children. She'd been a solemn, bookish nine years old at the time, given to daydreams and fairy tales.

Years later, after the last of the siblings had left the nest and she'd had time to think about such things, she had discovered somewhat to her surprise that buried under all those layers of enforced practicality, there still lurked a closet romantic who believed in charming princes and knights in shining armor.

Which might explain why she'd gone along with the fantasy when Vic had promised her the world with a cherry on top. His magicians had worked their magic, turning her into a glamorous stranger who wore exotic clothes and mingled with exotic people who owned yachts and who thought no more of flying over to Paris than she used to think about driving down to Brunswick or over to Waycross. Before she knew it, she'd found herself dreaming again about finding— Well, hardly a prince, but at least a special someone.

It hadn't happened. It wasn't going to happen. Mariah knew for a fact that there weren't any knights or princes waiting at Grover Shatley's Feed, Seed and Hardware. Muddy Landing didn't even boast a mayor, much less any royalty. The closest thing to a knight was Moe Chitty, who owned the town's only garage and had come to her rescue more than once when her car wouldn't start.

Blinking against the hypnotic spell of windshield wipers, Mariah shifted her position. Her legs were too long for a compact car, even with an adjustable seat—which hers no longer was. She should have taken a break before now, but the thought of jogging a few rounds at a rest stop in the pouring rain didn't particularly appeal.

Besides, she had too much on her mind. ''Maybe I just won't go back at all,'' she said out loud, voicing a thought that had been more and more in her mind this past month. Who needed New York? Who needed Palm Beach? Who needed her face on the cover of the Italian *Vogue*, anyway? Nobody in Muddy Landing had ever even heard of the rag, much less seen it.

Still, it paid awfully well. According to Kaye, fashion models weren't limited these days to walking a runway. One of Vic's girls had recently landed a small role in a soap opera, another had won an exclusive contract with a cosmetics firm.

It had seemed like a good idea at first, with no one at home depending on her. Seldom a month passed that one of her three sisters didn't call needing advice or a small loan. Financially, at least, her modeling career had been a godsend. Knowing that her family still depended on her in an emergency, she had saved every penny she could.

The trouble was, no matter how glamorous the life of a model looked from the outside, Mariah had never really gotten used to being treated like a side of beef—being handled, draped, pushed, pulled and spoken of as if she weren't even present by men who wore more jewelry and perfume than she ever had.

Selling hardware was a lot simpler. Muskrat traps, salt licks, well pumps and fescue seed. It was far from lucrative, but then, living in Muddy Landing didn't cost an arm and a leg, the way even breathing in Palm Beach or New York did.

Besides, she told herself as she squinted through the mixture of fog and rain for a sign of a service station, Muddy Landing was home. Be it ever so humble. Which it was. The glitzy life that had seemed so promising months ago had turned out to be mostly hard work, long hours, nastiness and one-upmanship.

Mariah flexed her shoulders, shifted on the rump-sprung bucket seat and glanced at the gas gauge. The needle nudged the empty mark and then bounced a zillionth of an inch. "Oh, Lordy," she muttered, searching the flat gray horizon for a faint gleam of neon. All she needed now was to run out of gas in the middle of I-95 in a cold, driving rain, with night coming on.

She took the first exit, but by the time she spotted the convenience store, her engine was beginning to cough. She flicked on her turn signal, praying that it still worked, and rolled off the highway onto the apron of the small store.

"Whew! Made it," she said with a sigh of relief.

Because she'd been lucky enough not to be stranded on the highway and because she was worried about Basil and Myrtiss and the baby, and was still undecided about her own future, Mariah decided to treat her car to a tankful of high-test, and herself to the biggest cherry drink she could find. And maybe a bag of boiled peanuts.

"And a rest room!" she added, shivering in the damp, chilly air. It had been warm enough when she'd set out, and she'd tossed her vinyl slicker and her white denim car coat into the back seat, then buried them under bags and boxes of cloths, books, curlers and makeup.

The rest rooms were inside, and as she had to pay before the attendant would turn on the gas pump, she made a dash for it, chill bumps covering her skin before she even made it through the door. After freshening up, she got her drink and peanuts and made her way to the counter. There was no one in the store except for the clerk and two grungy-looking men who were studying a girlie magazine rack near the counter. Wedging her way up beside them, she said, "Ten dollars' worth of gas, please. High-test."

Reluctantly the clerk turned away from the TV set. There was a basketball game under way. "That'll be ten for the gas, two-fifty for the peanuts, and with a Giant Freeze that comes to...lemmee see..."

Mariah plopped her purse on the counter beside her purchases, preparing to dig out her billfold. One of the two men abruptly left, letting in a blast of cold, wet air. She shivered. Just as the second man turned to follow, his elbow struck her drink, drenching her with the icy red liquid.

Mariah gasped. Appalled, she stared down at the spreading stain on her yellow linen pants and matching tunic and gingerly plucked the sodden fabric away from her body. Oh, blast! Why hadn't she taken the time to change into jeans? Now she was either going to have to dig out her suitcase and change clothes in the closet-size ladies' room, or drive the rest of the way home wet, cold and sticky.

Oh, fine. This was all she needed after rushing around all morning like a chicken drunk on sour mash, trying to tie up two dozen loose ends.

Get a grip, Mariah! You're supposed to be Fearless Leader.

That was what her younger siblings had always called her. Ha! If they'd only known what a fake she was.

"Hey, you!" yelled the clerk, and she glanced up in time to see the clumsy dolt who had drenched her running out the door—with her white shoulder bag under his arm!

It took a moment for it to sink in. "Stop him! You come back here!" she screamed. She lunged for the door, flinging out her hand to try to grab the flying strap of her purse.

Two things registered simultaneously as the door slammed shut on her fingers—the dark car that pulled up to the entrance, then sped off with a screech of rubber, and the pain that nearly brought her to her knees.

Clutching her right hand in her left one, Mariah shouldered open the door and barged into a solid wall of flesh. A tough-looking man with a black beard and a fierce scowl caught her by the shoulders.

"Get out of my way!" She shoved at him with both hands. Pain threatened to cripple her again.

"Whoa," the man growled. "What the hell's the big hurry?"

"Lady, you'll never catch him now. He's long gone," the attendant called after her.

Mariah ignored him. "Oh, God, he's getting away!" She dodged to the left just as the dark stranger did. She sidestepped right at the same time he did. The man's hands clamped down on her shoulders again, and Mariah glared at him, distractedly taking in the image of shaggy beard, battered, black leather jacket, rumpled khakis and worn Western boots. He looked unnaturally pale. "Would you please just let... me...*go?*" she wailed.

"What'd you do, rob the joint?"

The attendant stood behind her, surrounding her with his beer-and-onion breath. He squinted off into the veil of heavy rain. It was really pounding down now, dancing up off the pavement. A hundred-odd feet away, a steady stream of traffic raced by, headlights and taillights glowing fuzzily in the preternatural darkness. "Sorry, lady. They're long gone by now." He turned to go back inside, looking relieved that she instead of he had been the victim.

Breathing in a crazy mixture of lilacs, diesel fuel and cherry extract, Gus stared down at the woman in his arms. But not too far down, because she was almost as tall as he was.

Cheekbones. He'd always been a sucker for good bone structure. She had it. Man, did she ever have it! As long as she was there in his face, so to speak, he figured he might as well take inventory. He might be barely recovered from the lingering flu, but that didn't mean his male hormones were out of commission.

Her eyes were not quite brown, not quite gray—sort of a pale combination of the two. Her hair was the same no-color shade. Actually, she reminded him of a weimaraner that had taken up at his house a couple of years ago. He'd grown pretty fond of the mutt before the owner had finally shown up to claim him. "What happened?" he growled, wishing his voice didn't sound quite so rough. It hadn't been used much in the past week.

"That creep stole my purse! He poured Cherry Freeze all over me and then he grabbed my purse!" She tried to pull free, but Gus held on because, cheekbones or not, she looked pretty shaky. "Let me go! I've got to try and catch him!"

"Tall guy, short guy. Two of 'em. One had a baseball cap, the other one had sort of dirty blond hair and crooked teeth," the attendant said helpfully. "Didn't see no gun, but that don't mean nothing. Lot o' that kind o' thing going on these days."

The woman wilted visibly. For one brief moment she allowed her head to rest on Gus's leather-clad shoulder. "My keys," she whimpered. "He even has my car keys."

Gus glanced at the attendant, who hovered in the doorway. "Don't look at me, man, I can't leave this place. For what it's worth, they headed south in a dark Chevy—looked like a ten- to twelve-year-old model, but they're long gone by now. I'm real sorry, lady. You got any money on you? You still owe me for the drink and the—"

Gus swore. He jerked out his wallet and handed over a fistful of bills. "Take it out of that!"

While the two men were thus engaged, Mariah left the cover of the canopy. The rain had slacked up momentarily, and she'd spotted something pale and flat lying near the edge of the highway. It was probably only a bit of trash someone had tossed out, but . . .

Just as she reached the edge of the pavement, an eighteen-wheeler whipped past, throwing up a barrage of dirty water. She gasped at the second icy deluge within minutes.

"Are you crazy? Get the hell away from that highway, dammit!"

She just had time to snatch her purse when another truck roared past. Someone grabbed her hand—her left one, fortunately—and hauled her back from the edge of the highway. Before she could protest, her bearded assailant—or would-be rescuer—swung her off her feet and started jogging back toward the service station. "What the hell is it with you, lady? You got a death wish or something?"

He practically shoved her through the door before she could protest. The moment he set her on her feet again she tugged at the flap of her sodden purse, unthinkingly using her right hand.

Tears sprang to her eyes and she must have made a sound. Blackbeard took the dirty canvas shoulder bag from her, slung it over his own shoulder, and led her around behind the counter to the attendant's stool.

"Sit down before you fall down," he commanded. Very much to her surprise, she did. He handed over her purse. "I can tell you before you even look inside what you're going to find. Zilch. A lipstick, maybe a hanky, but nothing of value. Might as well face facts right up front."

Mariah glared at him, daring him to have spoken the truth.

But of course he had spoken only the truth. Gingerly, she held her ruined purse on her lap, wedging it under an elbow, and slid her left hand inside. Out came one sticky comb, one wad of damp, sticky tissues and a few sticky shards of the tiny jar of guava jelly she'd bought when she'd filled up her tank in West Palm. It had evidently broken and leaked all over the inside of her bag.

She didn't cry. Mariah never cried. Having learned a long time ago that tears were a waste of energy, she had developed her own way to deal with stress. If a few tears escaped now to slither down her rain-wet cheeks, that didn't mean she was crying. She would deal with this setback the way she had dealt with everything else since she had put away her dolls and taken on the job of raising a family.

Well . . . perhaps not exactly the same way. At least, not until she got home.

"What happened to your hand?" She glanced up as the pale-skinned, black-bearded stranger reached for her right hand, wondering if he was so pale because he'd just gotten out of prison. She wasn't ordinarily given to snap judgments, but it was hard not to be a little paranoid when she'd just been robbed and her hand was swollen, aching and rapidly turning an ugly shade of reddish purple.

It was also sticky.

Gus wiped his hand off on a clean handkerchief, wishing he'd never pulled off the highway for a break. Some break! He'd been feeling washed out, run down, mean as a junkyard dog—and that was before he'd had the misfortune to tangle with this particular walking disaster.

Oh, hell. The woman, her damp hair straggling around her wet face, was staring down at her own hand as if it belonged to someone else. If she hadn't looked so damned defeated, he might have been able to walk away. But Gus had always been a sucker for lost causes, and with those big, shimmering eyes and that naked, vulnerable mouth of hers, she was about as lost as it got.

"I'm going to wake up any minute now, and y'all are going to disappear. I just thought I ought to warn you." She tried to smile but her chin was trembling too hard. Her eyes were red-rimmed and the tip of her nose—her elegant, patrician nose, Gus noted almost absently—was beginning to turn pink.

Oboy. Here we go again.

Lilacs. She smelled like rain and lilacs. Backing away, he leaned against the snacks counter. If shadows had a color, that was the color of her eyes. The trouble was, even rimmed with red, they packed a wallop. And her legs— Oh, man, that was the clincher. Under a layer of thin, wet cloth, he could actually see the glow of her skin, the lines of her panties and bra. She didn't have a whole lot upstairs, but it was adequate. And it didn't take much imagination to tell that her nipples were all puckered up from the cold.

Why the hell wasn't she wearing a coat? "You ought to dress for the weather," he said gruffly, embarrassed at being caught staring at her body. He'd always had a weakness for her kind of looks, but when a guy was half dead from the flu, when he'd just been dumped by a woman he had actually bought a ring for, when his stomach was growling from hunger and acid was burning a hole in his gut, he had to be some kind of a pervert even to notice things like that.

Especially in a situation like this.

He made up for it by ratcheting up his scowl. "Look, this is Florida, lady, but let's get real. It's raining out there. It's February, it's cold as a well-digger's assets, and the overhead pipes have busted big-time. You got a coat somewhere?"

The attendant glanced out the clouded window as two cars pulled in. "Lady, you're gonna hafta move your car, okay? You're blocking the high-test."

"Shut up," Gus said without even glancing up. "What about a spare key? You got one stashed out someplace?"

"Under the hood, on the right side, on the thingamabob."

"The thingamabob. Right. Don't go away, I'll be right back."

And he was gone, leaving Mariah feeling lost and alone. Which wasn't like her at all. Ever since she'd answered the phone at four-thirty this morning and heard poor Basil's latest tale of woe, she seemed to have screwed up everything she touched. She was miles away from home and practically all the money she had in the world had been in her billfold; and now it was gone. She was wet, sticky and cold. The jet stream had moved south for the winter, and all her winter clothes were in the attic of her house back in Muddy Landing.

Truly, she'd had better days, she thought. When the bearded stranger came back inside, she tried to force a smile, but evidently it wasn't very convincing. He walked right up to her and clamped his big square hands on her upper arms and squeezed.

Hard.

"Here, I found this in your back seat. Better put it on before you catch something." He held out her vinyl slicker, and she slid her arms into the sleeves, wincing as the stiff plastic scraped her injured hand.

At that moment Mariah wanted nothing so much as to lean against the tough-looking stranger with the beard and the worn Western boots, close her eyes and forget everything. At least for a moment. For just a single minute, until she could think of what to do next.

Instead, she tilted her chin and tried to look as if she had everything under control. Which, evidently, was no more convincing than her smile had been.

He moved in closer until she could feel his heat, smell the mingled scent of leather and coffee and something essentially male. Which, oddly enough, was more reassuring than threatening.

"Hey, hey, now," he rasped. "It's not so bad. We'll get you sorted out in no time."

Two

Mariah made a real effort to pull herself together, if only because her bearded good samaritan seemed to expect it of her. She never liked to let anyone down, and besides—he was a lot kinder than he looked. Aside from that prison pallor of his and his shaggy beard, and the fact that he had a tendency to scowl a lot, he wasn't unattractive. Not handsome, certainly, but there was a rugged strength about him that was mighty appealing at the moment.

"I'll be fine," she murmured huskily. She fully intended to be, only it was going to take a bit of doing. "I'm just not used to being robbed," she said with a smile that was part bravado, part an effort at self-deception.

Turning away, she asked the clerk if she could use his telephone to call the police, not that she expected any results.

"Pay phone's outside next to the compressor," the attendant told her. She glared at him, and he had the grace to look embarrassed. Grudgingly, he indicated the private phone between the cash register and the jar of pickled eggs.

Dialing was a problem. Just one of several she was about to face, Mariah suspected, hanging up the phone a few minutes later.

The other man had gone outside again. He came in just as she was hanging up the phone, looking concerned under his intimidating scowl. "You got a name?" he asked.

"Mariah Brady."

"Gus Wydowski," he returned. "Look, Miss Brady, what about credit cards? If you had 'em, you might want to put in a stop call."

"Oh, Lord, my cards." She was beginning to tremble. Panic hovered just over the horizon.

"Driver's license, checkbook, keys..." He frowned, and Mariah wondered if he were capable of another expression.

"At least they headed south. I live north of here."

He nodded absently, his mind obviously miles away. Probably eager to be shed of her problems and be on his way. She noticed for the first time that his eyes were an unusual shade of dark blue, and that he had two scars on his face, one leading into his hairline, another disappearing under his beard.

"Were you carrying much cash?" he asked, and she was tempted to tell him it was none of his business, but she supposed she owed him a civil answer.

Her hand was beginning to throb painfully. "Don't ask," she said, which was about as civil as she could manage at the moment. She'd been carrying four hundred and seventy-three dollars and odd change. To some people, it might not be much. To Mariah, it was a fortune. Except for a minimum balance in her hometown bank, a five-thousand-dollar CD that wouldn't mature for several months and a run-down house in a tiny community where property values were a standing joke, it represented her entire life's savings.

It had been Vic Chin who had told her once that her face—or to be more precise, her bone structure—was her fortune. The trouble was, bone structure wouldn't pay the bills. Nor would it buy many groceries.

"How far are you going?" Gus Wydowski had a gruff way of speaking, almost as if his throat hurt.

"Muddy Landing," she said morosely. "It's in Georgia, near Darien."

"Near Darien. Right," he said, and she could tell from his tone that he'd never heard of Darien.

"Between Brunswick and Savannah, on the Little Charlie River," she elaborated. Actually, the Little Charlie was more of a creek, barely navigable since it had silted up. It was used mostly by trappers and fishing guides. The whole town had been built on a wetland before the Environment Protection Agency had even discovered wetlands, which was why property there was virtually worthless.

Gus was staring down at her swollen hand. Mariah stared, too. She could have cried—*would* have cried—if crying would have done any good. Some models she knew actually insured certain body parts. She pictured herself moving down the catwalk to the music, concentrating on every cue—smile here, open jacket here, pause here, drop stole and turn.

Great! Her jacket-opening hand was ruined. If she'd needed a sign, maybe this was it.

"You're going to have the devil of a time driving with that, you know."

She knew. She was going to have the devil of a time driving on an empty tank, too, but she didn't think their friend behind the counter would advance her much credit. *One cheekbone's worth of high-test, please?*

"I'll manage," she said, but Gus had already turned away. During the few moments it took him to stride down one aisle and up another, snatching a roll of paper towels and a box of plastic bags from the shelves, two women came in to use the rest room. Both stared at her curiously, and Mariah had an idea it was not because they recognized her from her brief career as a fashion model.

Gus ripped a plastic bag from the box, filled it at the ice machine, sealed it up and then tore open the roll of paper towels. A few long strides in the cluttered little store brought him back again, so close she could smell the leather of his coat and a hint of some smoky, spicy scent that reminded her of long-ago cookouts in the woods. If he wore a cologne, it wasn't obvious.

While she was still mentally comparing him to the overdressed, overscented men she had worked with for the past few months, he lifted her throbbing hand. She flinched, anticipating pain, but his touch was surprisingly gentle as he wrapped paper towels over the back of her hand. It was when he was folding the half-filled bag of ice around her swollen fingers that she noticed the fresh scar on the thumb side of his left hand. Swallowing a nervous urge to giggle, she said, "It looks like, between us, we have one good pair of hands."

He didn't even spare her a glance. "That hurt? Sorry. Ice'll take down some of the swelling. You allergic to aspirin?"

She shook her head. "No. That is, yes, I know it will, and no, I'm not."

He pulled a tin of tablets from his shirt pocket, dumped two into her free hand and another two into his own. Then he got two drinks from the cooler, twisted off the tops and handed her one.

It was lemon-lime. She didn't like lemon-lime, but she drank it anyway, to wash down the painkiller.

"Got a proposition for you," he said, and she waited warily. "The way I see it, you're in no shape to drive, even if you had a driver's license. You really ought to see a doctor about that hand, and—"

"No. No, thank you."

"If it's broken—"

"It's not." She couldn't afford for it to be broken, not with Basil bringing the baby down from Atlanta on Saturday. Couldn't afford it, period.

"Don't get your back up so fast. Just hear me out, okay?"

"Look, I'll stop off and see a doctor on the way home, all right? And while I appreciate all you've done, Mr. Wydowski, I really don't need your help."

He muttered something under his breath, and Mariah was just as glad she hadn't heard him clearly. He stared at her for the longest time, making her acutely aware of her lank, wet hair, her damp, stained clothes under the stiff vinyl coat, and the fact that whatever makeup she had started out with that morning had long since been rained off, chewed off and otherwise eroded.

Shoulders sagging, Mariah thought that if she'd needed a reminder of who she was and where she belonged, this did the job. Underneath the glossy finish, she was still plain old Sara Mariah Brady, perennial baby-sitter, bespectacled beanpole who, until at the advanced age of twenty-five, she'd made a fool of herself over Vance Brubaker, had been the oldest living virgin in captivity. At least in Muddy Landing.

Evidently, the man read body language. He'd probably known the moment he heard her sigh, saw her sagging shoulders, that she was no match for him. "Go ahead and say what you're thinking," she said dully. "I'm listening."

Which was how she came to find herself a short while later in a motel room somewhere near Saint Augustine. The police had come and gone, for all the good it had done. Her car was back at the gas station, parked in an out-of-the-way spot. Gus had tossed everything from her back seat into the surprisingly ample space behind the seat of his truck.

"What the hell do you have in here, bricks?" he grumbled, carting the last of the boxes into her room.

"Do you have something against bricks?"

He sent her a sour look, and she was reminded that he had an injured hand, too. "It's books," she said. "You didn't have to bring all that stuff. It would've been all right in the car until morning."

"Do you have a phone credit ca—" Gus caught himself. Of course she didn't have a phone credit card. It had gone the way of all her other credit cards. "Make whatever calls you need from the room, okay?" He tried to sound gracious, but gracious wasn't his style.

He could have been halfway down the coast by now, but, dammit, he couldn't just drive off and leave her to spend the night where she was. That creep in the service station would have charged her for the floor space she took up. He'd charged for leaving her clunker there overnight, for the plastic bags and the paper towels and the drinks. Gus knew damned well she'd been mentally running a tab while he was settling up with the guy. She'd asked him to write down his address so she would know where to send the money.

He'd seen the look on her face when he'd hauled out one of his business cards. What the devil did she take him for, a bum? Was she afraid he was going to hit on her? Was that why she was so worried?

Because she was worried, all right, and he had a feeling it was more than just getting mugged. That little ditto mark between her eyebrows wasn't due to an excess of happy thoughts.

Gus did his best not to look at her any more than he could help, on account of he liked what he saw too much. It was a good thing she'd kept her raincoat on, because in spite of a few superficial deficiencies of a strictly temporary nature, she was something else. Not exactly drop-dead gorgeous. Not even pretty, in the usual sense. The trouble was, she had the kind of timeless beauty he'd always been a sucker for.

"Maybe you'd better start calling a few people. Family, husband, that kind of thing, but if you want my advice, you'll call first and put a stop on your credit cards before you find yourself in real trouble."

"Real trouble?" she asked, a brittle edge to her voice that Gus didn't like, not one bit. "You mean the kind I'm in now isn't real? You know, I did think for a few minutes there that I might be dreaming."

As a joke, it wasn't even in the running, but he gave her high marks for trying. Maybe after a night's sleep and a good meal, they'd both feel better. "Hey, are you as hungry as I am? I skipped a few meals today."

"Thanks, but I'm not at all—"

"Piece of pie might lift your spirits," he tempted. He could have reminded her that she was in hock so deep now that the price of a meal wasn't going to make that much difference, but he didn't.

"Actually, now that you mention it, I'm ravenous," she admitted.

He found himself dangerously close to liking her. Studying her with the practiced eye of a connoisseur, Gus summed up what he saw. Five-ten, ten-and-a-half, about 112 pounds. A size six, he figured. Lisa was a size eight. This woman was smaller boned. Almost fragile.

Back off, man! You've taken the cure, remember?

"So what'll it be, steak? Seafood?" he prompted.

"I had a bag of boiled—"

"Peanuts. Right. They're on top of the box of bricks. Look, why don't I check with the desk and see what's available around these parts while you make your calls? I'm in the room next door. Just bang on the wall when you're ready."

Gus walked out and slammed into his own room next door, thinking about all the times he'd stopped to pick up a stray mutt and ended up with a stack of vet's bills and a houseful of fleas, not to mention a few bites. He took the time to shower and change into clean khakis and a black knit shirt. Fortunately, his favorite boots were past the polishing stage. He kept them dressed with wet-proofing, so they still looked pretty good to his way of thinking.

He wondered if his effort to look respectable would reassure the skittish woman in the room next door. He was already beginning to regret the impulse that had made him take on her case. Maybe he should have just bought her a tank of gas, wished her well and kept on going. Unfortunately, that hadn't been an option. Even feeling like hell warmed over, strung out on caffeine, sugar and aspirin, all it had taken was one look at those stricken eyes of hers and he'd gone down for the count.

At least he could take comfort in knowing she wasn't on the road with a busted mitt and no driver's license, trying to make Georgia on a dark, rainy night. Although, grimacing at his shaggy image in the mirror as he collected his wallet, keys and pocket change, Gus couldn't say much for the judgment of any woman who would meekly allow a stranger to drive her to the nearest motel, no matter how innocent the situation appeared on the surface.

He stroked his beard. One of these days he was going to have to take the time to get himself trimmed up. Lisa had tried more than once to talk him into shaving, back in the honeymoon stage of their relationship, but he'd held out. Probably, he admitted now, because he'd been afraid she wouldn't like what she saw.

Maybe if he got hot enough down on that sun-drenched beach that was just waiting for him somewhere south of here—a beach where he didn't know a bloody soul and nobody knew him—he might even decide to get reacquainted with his own face. At the moment, however, he needed all the cover he could get.

Sooner or later, Gus told himself as he let himself out the door, he was going to have to kick a few bad habits. Number one was being unable to say no to a lady—canine, feline or otherwise. Just last summer he'd found himself giving aid and comfort—not to mention room and board—to a one-eared cat and her litter of kittens, two half-starved pups that had been dumped on a country road and a raccoon that was so old and blind she'd fallen out of a persimmon tree and knocked herself out. Eventually, he'd managed to find them all permanent homes.

With women, his record wasn't quite so good. The first woman he'd ever loved—or thought he did—had ended up marrying his best friend. He'd been young and idealistic, and it had taken him a while to get over it, but he'd survived. There'd been other women since then—a lot of them, because Gus truly enjoyed women. But he didn't date anyone seriously. Not until Lisa, and maybe not even then.

The trouble was, the kind of woman he was hooked on never quite lived up to his expectations. Eventually he'd learned not to expect anything.

And no matter what Mariah looked like—no matter how much she engaged his sympathy—she was not going to get to him. No way! All he had to do was ignore those big weimaraner eyes and that long, lean, languorous body of hers for a few more hours. Come morning, he would drop her off at her car, treat her to a tank of gas and send her on her way with his blessings.

And then he'd head south and continue his quest for the sun. There damn well had to be a sun out there somewhere!

It was still coming down like Niagara Falls when Mariah let herself out a few minutes later. Gus took one look at her and then hurried out to unlock the truck.

Down, boy. Think big, juicy steak. Think pecan pie smothered with ice cream . . . think anything but what you're thinking!

The lady cleaned up real good. She was wearing jeans, a man's white shirt, vinyl slicker and a pair of cork-soled sandals that towered about three inches off the ground, making those skyscraper legs of hers even more spectacular. She looked like a million bucks. But then, even wet, stained, bruised and swollen, she'd rated well over the top on any man's gauge.

Gus figured the sooner they parted ways, the better. "Steak, seafood, waffles or burgers, take your pick. There's a chicken takeout three miles farther down the road." He did his best to ignore the way she got into a truck. Mariah was tall enough to edge her hip onto the seat and swing both legs inside in one smooth, flowing motion.

He closed the door and stalked around the hood. Dammit, it was going on nine and his last meal had been a candy bar a couple of hundred miles ago. "Make up your mind," he said, his voice rough from an earlier bout of coughing.

"I'm not real crazy about waffles. Anything else suits me, though. You choose."

Following the directions he'd received from the night clerk, Gus drove to the steak house. The waiting line stretched all the way out to the edge of the canopy. Without a word he backed out and headed for the two closest seafood places, only to discover that the shortest wait at either place would be at least an hour.

"Goodness, I wonder what it's like on a weekend," Mariah murmured. Her stomach growled noisily.

"This is Florida, right? It's February, so what d'you expect?" He was hungry, too, but it was hard to feel too grim when he was this close to a woman who turned him on big time without even trying. Which was crazy, because he wasn't even over his last affair! At least, he hadn't thought he was. But there was something downright disarming about a growling stomach on a woman who looked like the cover of a six-dollar fashion magazine, even in a plastic raincoat.

They drove a few miles farther, picked up a couple of chicken dinners and headed back to the motel. Gus eased into the parking place, then leaned across and opened her door, trying hard to ignore the mingled smell of fried chicken, lilacs and warm woman. He tucked the boxes under his coat and made a dive for the shelter.

Mariah was right beside him, her wet face and wet slicker glistening under the security lights. She was laughing, but Gus noticed she was supporting her right hand with her left. He knew from personal experience that two hands were better than one, especially for things like opening chicken boxes and shucking plastic utensils out of their packets.

And hell, it wasn't as if he had anything better to do.

While the rain droned down a few feet away, he watched her struggle to unlock her door left-handed, then impatiently took the key and did the job for her. She wasn't a whiner, he would give her that much.

"Thanks," she murmured. "And, Gus, thank you for supper." She lifted a box off the stack and stepped inside. "I'll add it to my account."

Gus was going to say "You do that" when his throat betrayed him again. His cough, a remnant of the flu, sounded a lot worse than it was.

"That sounds awful! Come inside for a minute, I might have something…" She had that same mother-hen glint in her eye his sister Angel always got when she was trying to cure his sweet tooth. "I know I've got something in one of my bags—everybody's been coughing lately."

Nearly strangling, Gus followed her inside. Even with his eyes watering, he couldn't help but appreciate her rear end as she leaned over to fumble left-handed through the bottles, jars and tubes in her makeup case. "Hey, don't go to any trouble on my account," he rasped. "I never take medicine."

She pulled out a card of foil-wrapped lozenges and held it out to him. "Yes, you do. I saw you take aspirin earlier, remember?"

"That's not medicine, that's— Ah, hell, give me the thing," he snapped, and immediately regretted his surliness. "Sorry. It's been a long day."

"It has, hasn't it?" There was no reproach in her voice, but her quiet Georgia accent made him feel about the size of a small cockroach. "I expect you're hungry, too. Why don't we have supper and make an early night of it? I have a long drive ahead of me tomorrow, and you probably do, too. Where are you going, anyway?"

As she was making a real mess of trying to open a chicken box one-handed, Gus took it from her and finished the job. With a courtly gesture, he pulled out her chair, partly to make up for being a sorehead. *Play it cool, man. This is strictly business. Ships in the night, and all that.* "Wait here. I'll get us something to drink. You want cold from the machine, or coffee?"

"Cold, please. Diet cola's fine."

"Chemicals are bad for you. Sugar's real food."

She smiled, and it occurred to him as he dug in his pocket for change that if she smiled much more, there was no telling how big a fool he was going to make of himself before he managed to get away.

Awkwardly, she set out the napkins and plastic cutlery. "Don't go to any trouble," Gus warned. "I can eat in my own room."

"Yes, but if you stay here you can have my biscuit and the wing on my breast quarter. I never eat wings."

"Are you trying to bribe me?"

"Not at all. Call it a down payment on what I owe you. Did you order the potatoes and gravy, or the fries?"

"There's one of each, take your choice," he said, and she smiled again. He wondered if she was coming on to him.

She wasn't. He wasn't quite sure how he knew—he just knew. There was nothing at all flirtatious about the way she picked up her chicken breast in her left hand and bit into it. Hell, she probably wasn't any more anxious to get involved than he was, he told himself, wondering why the thought wasn't more reassuring.

Gus knew for a fact that some women took one look at his battered face, scarred from one too many football collisions and the usual run of on-the-job accidents, and took a fast hike. But just because this one hadn't, didn't mean she was feeling the same pull of sexual attraction he was feeling.

And he was definitely, undeniably feeling it, all right. It was a good thing they would be splitting pretty soon, or else Gus might just find himself forgetting a few hard-learned lessons from his own recent past.

Three

———

Dinner was devoured quickly, with little conversation. Mariah told herself there was nothing at all wrong with finding herself alone in a motel room in a strange town with a strange man. It happened.

A small inner voice, one she had never quite managed to outgrow, whispered that it might happen to some women; it had certainly never happened to Sara Mariah Brady.

As a model, Mariah's social life had been even more limited than it had been back home, if for an entirely different reason. The novelty of beautiful clothes, beautiful people and exotic locations had quickly worn off. After initial training, her days had begun early, and by the time she'd gotten back to the apartment all she'd wanted to do was devour an enormous meal and fall into bed.

Instead, she usually made do with a quick shower—cool, so as not to dry out her skin—a manicure touchup, half an hour of yoga and a light supper of fruit, rice and vegetables. *Then* she would fall into bed.

Back in Muddy Landing the store had closed at five in the wintertime, six during the summer. By the time she'd cooked supper for whoever happened to be living at home, she'd been tired, but not too tired to have gone out for a few hours if anyone had asked her.

The trouble was, in Muddy Landing, there was no "out" to go to. Nor was there anyone to go with once she'd discovered that Vance Brubaker, charming, attentive sales rep for a garden tractor manufacturer, had four motherless children at home, and was seeing a woman in Darien and one in Wayne County at the same time he was courting Mariah, in the hopes that one of the three would be willing to take on his family. Nor did he particularly care which one. Mariah had almost convinced herself she was in love with the man when the whole affair had started to come unraveled.

Sighing, she finished supper and deftly closed the remains inside her box with her left hand. "I never knew I was ambidextrous." It was the first thing either of them had said since Gus had opened her salt and pepper packets and she'd thanked him.

"Good thing you are. Let's see about getting that mitt of yours iced down again before I leave you."

Thunder and lightning had set in about half an hour earlier. Now a blast of thunder rattled the windows, making her flinch. "Actually, I'm not all that sleepy. I wonder if there's a weather channel we could tune in to."

There was. While Mariah washed her hands, then studiously stared at all the L's, the H's and the curving dotted lines on the weather map, Gus filled the ice tub from the machine outside.

"What's the prognosis?" he asked when he came back inside. He refilled the bag, arranged her right hand on the chair arm, spread a small towel over the swollen bruise and then carefully placed the ice bag in position, trying not to admire her graceful, long-fingered hands too much. Trying not to let his imagination run away with him.

"Prognosis? Oh, the weather, you mean. I forgot to listen."

The truth was, Mariah had been too busy thinking about Gus. Wondering who he was. Where he was from. Why he was traveling alone.

To a job, perhaps. Maybe he was looking for work. She'd spent hours in his company, yet she didn't know the first thing about him except that despite his rough looks, the semipermanent scowl that was etched on his bearded face and the pallor she had first taken for something sinister, he was kind. Most men would have walked away long before this, but for some reason he seemed determined to help her.

Whether she wanted him to or not! "Gus, where are you headed?"

The narrowed glance he sent her way spelled Keep Out in dark, electric blue. "South," he said tersely.

Removing the bag, he unzipped it, popped out a few cubes, resealed and replaced it.

"I'm going home to Georgia," she confided. "I guess I already told you about Muddy Landing, didn't I?"

"Yep." He stepped back to frown down at her, his fists bracing a pair of narrow hips. "Need a couple more aspirin before you turn in?"

"If I do, I'm sure I have some somewhere." He obviously wanted to get away. That, for some reason, irritated her. After protesting her independence earlier, for all the good it had done her, she was suddenly in no mood to be alone.

Too much to think about. Too many questions with no answers that she'd just as soon put off asking as long as she could. Which wasn't like her at all.

But then, nothing about this whole messy business was typical of the practical, unflappable woman she'd always been. While finishing high school, holding down a part-time job and later, a full-time one, all the while taking care of her siblings, Mariah had dealt with every childhood disaster imaginable.

Of course, she'd had her own method of dealing with stress in those days. Digging. Planting and transplanting. There were too many things in her life she couldn't change, so she changed the things she could. Rearranging furniture had never given her half the satisfaction that rearranging shrubbery had. She had the greenest thumbs in Muddy Landing—everybody said so—but Basil had once told her that all she had to do was step outside the back door with a certain look on her face, and every shrub in the yard flinched.

Lately, she'd had to make do with yoga.

"Well ... good night, Gus. And thank you for my supper and the room. And all the rest. Naturally, I'll mail you a check just as soon as—"

"Yeah, sure," was the gruff response.

The man was a bear. If it weren't for those remarkably beautiful eyes of his, he wouldn't even rate a second glance, she told herself, stung by the fact that he could obviously hardly wait to get away.

Oh, yes, he would, too. In spite of surface appearances, the man radiated authority. He was intensely masculine. And while some women might be put off by the beard and all that shaggy black hair, with those wide shoulders and narrow hips, and those strong, amazingly gentle hands, he most definitely rated a second look.

Maybe even a third.

And that was not even taking into account what a thoroughly nice man he was underneath his grizzly bear disguise.

"I left a call for both rooms for seven. Is that too early?"

"Seven's fine," she assured him. "I always get up early."

"Yeah, sure you do," he growled.

His skepticism irritated her, but Mariah put it down to the weather. Thunderstorms always made her edgy. "For your information, Mr. Wydowski—"

"It's Gus. Or plain Wydowski."

"Well, for your information, Plain Wydowski, I'm used to working a minimum of twelve hours a day." Which was no less than the truth, if one included marketing, personal laundry and her grooming and exercise routine. Or holding down a full-time job in addition to keeping house. "You'd think I did nothing but loll about half the day eating Twinkies and reading juicy horror stories."

"How about boiled peanuts and romances?" Was there the suspicion of a twinkle in his eyes? Probably just a reflection of the lightning. "Seven it is, then," he said, letting himself out the brick red door just as a blast of thunder exploded overhead.

Nursing the slippery ice bag, Mariah wasted no time on indignation. She had a lot of worrying to do and she needed to organize it into manageable lots. Money was the first problem. She would have to cash in her CD. The penalty couldn't be all that much, but at the moment she didn't have a single dollar to spare. Her health insurance was due and she'd have to stock up on supplies, including baby food and diapers and whatever else an eight-month-old baby needed. Knowing Basil, it would never occur to him to bring them along.

Just as it hadn't occurred to him that Mariah's work was every bit as important as his own—that she couldn't just walk away when it suited her.

Yes, well . . . she had, hadn't she? Which was another problem.

Nor had it occurred to her brother that she'd had absolutely no experience with infants. Rosemary had been three when their mother had more or less abdi-

cated her role, Alethia nearly five, Burdina six and
Basil nearly eight. Mariah, as the eldest, had taken
over and looked after them all until the last one had
left the nest.

They were all more or less settled now. Rosemary
was training to be a nurse, Alethia working for an insurance firm in Decatur, Burdina was in her third year
at Emory. Burdy had always been the brainy one. She
had earned a full scholarship. And then there was
Basil, with a family and a business of his own in Atlanta.

But they still needed her. Seldom a week went by
that she didn't hear from at least one of them, and as
often as not they needed something, if only a small
loan.

Mariah, as tired as she was, felt a small glow of satisfaction. It was nice to be needed. Exhausting but
nice.

Outside, the thunderstorm was in full spate, the
noise nearly drowning out the sound of the rain. Inside, the TV set droned on and on. A perky young
man in a bow tie cheerfully described the probable ef-
fects of the southward swoop of the northern jet
stream. Rain with the possibility of a few flurries unless something or other happened, in which case, the
flurries might add up to one to three inches of frozen
precipitation.

Lord ha' mercy, if that wasn't just what she needed!
It didn't snow often, which made it worse when it did.
Nobody was prepared. Oh, for a shovel and a few
shrubs to transplant.

As she couldn't change the forecast, Mariah did the next best thing. She switched channels to a movie that featured a ride-'em-down, shoot-'em-up Western. At least the noise of that, plus the thunder, drowned out her own nonproductive thoughts. Clutching the ice bag to her injured hand, she began to pace. On the thin carpet, her platform sandals made a satisfying clunking sound.

In the room next door Gus tried to concentrate on the newspaper he'd brought from home, but yesterday's news might as well have been written about a different planet. What the hell was he doing in a cheap motel in the pouring down rain, somewhere in northern Florida, anyway? He'd been headed for sunshine. For summertime. All the way to Key West if that was where he had to go to find it!

And what the bloody hell was she doing in there? he asked himself, glaring at the thin wall that separated the two rooms. Guns blazed, cattle stampeded, and now she was stomping around in those godawful shoes of hers that made her a full inch taller than he was.

Gus told himself she'd probably worn them deliberately. He was wise to women and the little tricks they used to manipulate men.

Well, let her tower over him—he didn't give a sweet damn in hell. His manhood wasn't threatened by a woman who could look him in the eye. He might still be half dead with the flu, but his manhood was alive and well, thanks. He'd already had evidence of that fact.

Women! It would serve her right if he dumped her out at the station, bought her a tankful of gas, and took off. It was no skin off his nose if she had to drive one-handed all the way to Newfoundland. At least then he would be able to get his mind on track again and keep it there.

Maybe if he put in a call to his sister, she could set him on course again. Angel had always been good at putting him in his place and making him laugh about it. She was the only family he had left—the most important person in his life.

But Angel had her own life now. She and Alex were expecting their first kid in June. Which would make him an uncle. Which was something, at least, only suddenly, unclehood didn't seem all that fulfilling.

Clump, clump, clump. Bang, screech, clump! He could pound on the wall, but she would never hear him over all that ruckus. If those walls had passed muster with any inspector, Gus couldn't say much for the building code in this neck of the woods.

And then in a rare moment of silence came the sound of breaking glass, followed by a shrill little yelp. He had a gut feeling it wasn't a part of any TV Western. Pausing only long enough to grab his room key, Gus barged out the door of 102 and beat on the door of 103. Getting no results, he moved to the wide window, wiped off the glass and peered through a crack in the draperies.

She was standing there, stiff as a stalking heron, near the back of the room. God, she was something to look at, even with one towel-draped hand clutched to her chest, the other one hanging on to the plastic handle of a broken coffee maker. There were shards of glass around her feet, and—

And she was crying. Oh, hell. No way could he walk now. Tomorrow he would cut his losses and get the hell out of range, but right now...

It took rapping on the glass with his pocketknife before she even glanced his way. She blinked a few times and he watched her visibly pull herself together. Tears and a busted fist notwithstanding, this was one feisty broad.

"Did you want something?" she inquired coolly through the crack in the door.

"Unhook the chain."

"I don't—"

"Mariah, unhook the chain, please." If he had to, he would manufacture another coughing spell. Come to think of it, he probably wouldn't have to try too hard. His throat still felt as if it were lined with double-ought sandpaper.

She let him in and then stood by, her face expressionless, while he switched off the TV. Next, he found a wastebasket and began gathering up broken glass. "How the devil can you hear yourself think with all that noise?" he grumbled.

"Maybe I didn't want to hear myself think."

"Yeah, well, maybe I did."

"I'm not stopping you. Go home and think all you want to, I don't need you to clean up after me."

She sounded so damned haughty, standing there in her skinny jeans and her baggy shirt. Damned if she didn't have a rumpled tea bag dangling from her little finger. Gus had to grin. *Lady, you don't even know when you're down for the count, do you?*

"Where'd you get the tea bag?" he asked gruffly, smothering an urge to laugh.

"I found it in my coat pocket."

"Looks like it's left over from last season. Got any coffee stashed away there?"

"It wouldn't do you any good. In case you hadn't noticed, I broke my pot." There'd been a wall-mounted coffee maker in each room, but no coffee. But then, this was not exactly a top-of-the-line establishment.

"Stay put. I'll get my mine."

He was back in less than a minute. She hadn't moved an inch. Gus had an idea she was hanging in there against some pretty stiff odds, which meant he was probably slated to put in a few hours of listening while she dragged out her worries and hung them out to dry. For some reason he'd never been able to figure out, women always seemed to want to confide in him.

His sister, Angel, said it was because he looked older than his years, and age was an indication of wisdom. Gus hadn't been particularly flattered, but then, Angel had never been one to sugarcoat the truth. With a few choice words he'd told her what he'd thought of her theory, but it had started him to thinking about growing old. More specifically, about growing old alone.

Which was probably why he'd even considered asking Lisa to marry him. Up until then he'd liked his life fine just the way it was.

He was just beginning to realize what a narrow escape he'd had. Looking back on a few of Lisa's more irritating little habits, such as being uninterested in any conversation that wasn't focused on herself, Gus figured he'd got off lucky. He could glance at a blueprint and size up a job within minutes, but when it came to reading women, he still had a few blind spots. So much for age and wisdom.

The water came to a boil. Gus turned to where Mariah stood, still dangling her mangled tea bag. "Where's your cup?"

"I thought . . . the glass?"

At least it was glass, not plastic. Gus took the bag from her finger and dropped it into one of the room's two glasses, then poured boiling water slowly down the side until the glass was full. He got a washcloth from the bathroom and wrapped the glass before handing it over.

"Go sit down before you drop," he said. She was looking a little too pale to suit him.

"You do that so well, you must be an expert."

"Do what, make tea?"

"Order people around."

"Oh. That."

Except for the drone of rain, it was quiet. The TV was silent; the thunder had moved on. Gus hooked the toe of his boot around the other chair, dragged it closer and sat down. "So . . . let's have it. What's got you so all-fired worried you're trying to drown out your own thoughts with a high-decibel cow opera?"

"I don't know what gives you the idea that I'm—"

He cut her off at the pass. "If you want some sugar for that tea, I've probably got a few packets in the truck."

She shook her head. "I like it bitter. How's your cough?"

"Fine. Come on, lady—give. What's got you strung up tighter than a two-dollar fiddle?"

"I don't know what you're talking about," she said brightly. Too brightly. "Do you mean aside from the fact that some creep stole practically every cent I have in the world and I can't use my right hand, and I'm miles from home and my car's out of gas, and Basil's coming home on Saturday with his baby daughter, expecting me to take care of her until he can find Myrtiss and talk her into going back home? Because outside that, I don't have a single worry."

Gus stared at her for the longest time, for once oblivious to her classical cheekbones, her flawlessly sculpted nose, a pair of spectacular eyes and a chin that had a tendency to square up at the least hint of a challenge.

"Uh-huh," he said dryly. "That'd just about do it, I guess."

He didn't have the foggiest notion who Basil and Myrtiss and their baby were, or what they had to do with Mariah, but if there was one thing he was, it was a damn good listener. He told her so.

She sighed, nursing her glass of tea. "Well, there's my job, too. I mean, if I decide to go back. And if I don't, I'm not sure I can find anything else. I'll have to do something, but there's not a lot of choice in Muddy Landing, or even in Darien. And even if I wanted to sell the house and move somewhere else, I couldn't. It needs too much work. It's been listed to rent for nearly a year with no takers. I'd never find a buyer, even if it weren't in a floodplain.''

Gus stroked his beard. He tried to look thoughtful, as if he knew precisely what she was talking about and was halfway to coming up with a solution. "You, uh, didn't mention what it is that you do in this Muddy Landing of yours."

''I was the assistant manager for Grover Shatley's Feed, Seed and Hardware Emporium. It's the largest business in town. I worked there for nearly twelve years, until just a few months ago.''

If she'd said she worked in an iron foundry, he wouldn't have been any more surprised. "Did you quit or were you fired?''

''I left to try something else, but I think I like my old job better. Unfortunately, Grover replaced me, but even before I left there was talk of the store's closing down, which was one of the reasons I decided to take a chance on something else. A... a career move, I suppose you could call it. Only it didn't work out quite like I expected. I guess I'm not cut out for city life.''

Waitress, Gus thought. Maybe a receptionist. She'd sure dress up any office, and he had an idea she had a few more brains than he'd given her credit for.

Come to think of it, she could easily make it as a model if she wanted to. Maybe he ought to suggest it. He could give her the name of the agency Lisa had gone with.

Sprawled in one of the room's two chairs, Gus propped his chin on his knuckles and surveyed the woman in front of him. No doubt about it, she'd look right at home in a fashion spread in one of those glossy magazines Lisa used to devour. Which was pretty damned ironic, come to think of it. Here he was, alone with a gorgeous, long-legged woman in a motel room on a night that was made for romance and—

Romance, hell! It was made for trouble, he thought ruefully. Lucky for him he'd already promised himself that if he ever, *ever* got involved with another woman, she would be short, dumpy, freckled and plain as a mud fence. The kind of woman who hadn't grown up trading on her looks to the point where she'd never developed much beyond adolescence. From now on his requirements included sensible, reasonably intelligent and good-natured. Looks came pretty far down on the list.

Of course, she would have to be willing to put up with him, too, which might be a problem.

Gus had never kidded himself that he was any great prize. Oh, he was smart enough, even though he'd dropped out of college just short of a degree. He owned his own business and could pretty well call the shots. He'd never been arrested—although there had been a few close calls back in his hell-raising football days. He went to church now and then, mostly for the music and because he liked the architecture. He donated regularly to several charities. He was moderate in his habits, except for a few minor weaknesses such as the one that had triggered his present troubles.

Which, come to think of it, didn't seem all that troubling any more. He drew a deep, satisfying breath and let it out in a relaxing sigh.

The rain continued to drone down all around them, enclosing them in a small, cozy space. Mariah sighed in response to Gus's sigh. She'd spent years learning to read her siblings in order to head off their more foolhardy impulses. Maybe it was the beard, but she found Gus a lot harder to read. She was pretty sure he didn't want to be here, at least not with her, yet he seemed resigned to shouldering her burdens.

Amused, she told herself that he definitely had the shoulders for it, if not the disposition. All things considered, Gus Wydowski was a very nice man. She wondered when the last time was that anyone had told him so.

In the oddly intimate circumstances, she found herself wondering a lot of things about the man who had so unexpectedly intruded into her life.

Or had she intruded into his?

Either way, in just a few short hours she had caught glimpses of a complex and lonely man underneath that rugged exterior. It was those glimpses that were beginning to intrigue her to the point where, with a little encouragement, she just might dredge up a few of her old half-forgotten fantasies.

Lord ha' mercy, that would never do! There was a time and a place for everything, and this was definitely neither.

Still, she couldn't help but wonder if he was married. "I told you all about my life, now it's your turn," she said. Actually, she hadn't mentioned the modeling, but then, she'd been a model for less than a year. She'd done the other for practically all her life.

Gus wasn't paying much attention to her words; he was too busy thinking of all the clichés he'd ever heard about a woman's skin.

Silk.

Flower petals.

Ivory.

They all applied. Was it his imagination, or was there enough sexual tension sizzling around this place to power a small town? If she didn't feel it, then her insulation must be a damned sight more effective than his was.

Or maybe she was just smarter than he was. It was a fluke, their even being here like this. The whole situation was too bizarre to be taken seriously. In a few hours they'd part company and never see each other again, which was a damned good thing because evidently all this rain had shorted out a few important circuits in his brain.

"Gus?"

"Hmm?"

"I asked what you did for a living."

"What? Oh. I'm a builder, like it said on my business card. ATW Construction." She smelled of lilacs. He'd always had a weakness for lilacs. His Aunt Zee had had two big lilac bushes in her backyard, and in the springtime the scent filled the whole neighborhood.

And, God, she was graceful! Mariah—not Aunt Zee. She had a way of sitting, even in a cheap, plastic, motel chair, that made the most of her assets. The way her legs were twined around each other was something else!

"Is that what you're on your way to do? I thought most of the post-hurricane rebuilding was already done."

Gus had never been much good at small talk. Nor was he good at confiding. Even his best friend knew better than to push too hard. This woman—this stranger—this elegant waif with the soft, husky voice and those big, shadow-colored eyes—was beginning to get under his skin.

He shifted position and at the same time reined in his sexual interest. "I'm on vacation. The weather's been lousy, and I'm between projects, so I'm taking a few days off, okay? You got a problem with that?"

Gus could have kicked himself. He was a little short on social skills—hell, he was a lot short. All the same, he'd never made a habit of cutting people up into small pieces.

"Sorry," he said, and meant it. He wasn't much on apologizing, either, but she didn't deserve the raw edge of his tongue. "This weather's beginning to get to me. I had the flu recently, too—not that that's any excuse for lousy manners."

"Yes, it is. I'm always cross when I have a cold. My family tiptoes and whispers around the house, but mostly they stay out of my way."

Her family. Gus sighed. He didn't want to know anything more about her. There was no reason to get too cozy—they weren't going to be buddies, and they sure as hell weren't going to be anything else! But in an effort to make up for biting her head off, he asked about her family and learned that she wasn't married. Not that he cared one way or another, only if there was a husband somewhere in the background, allowing her to run around loose this way—to go to motels with strange men—then he was a fool who deserved to lose her.

She told him about her brother, sisters, sister-in-law and the niece she was going home to look after. He found out more than he really cared to know about Basil's struggling new computer consulting business that took eighteen out of every twenty-four hours, and about Myrtiss's resentment at having to do book-keeping at home for Basil's business and several others, and at the same time, to keep house and look after a baby with too little help from her husband.

In return, and because he had no intention of telling her anything personal, Gus shared a few zany occurrences from the building business, such as the investment broker who had handed over a set of blueprints, a check big enough to choke a camel, and announced that he was setting out to sail around the world. When he got back, he intended to move into his house. When Gus had wanted to go over the plans with him, he'd flatly refused. "I designed it myself. There's nothing that needs discussing. Just build it precisely the way I planned it, period. That's what I'm paying you for."

So Gus and his crew had followed the plans faithfully, and the broker had come home eleven months later to a two-story house with no stairway.

Mariah had laughed until tears ran down her cheeks. For a woman with the kind of looks that could only be described as elegant, if not downright aristocratic, she had a surprisingly earthy laugh. Gus laughed, too, and it occurred to him that his chest was no longer quite so congested. His throat felt a hell of a lot better, too, come to think of it.

Yeah, they'd talked. She was interesting. Just off-beat enough so that he couldn't quite figure out where she was coming from.

But that didn't mean he was going to take on her problems. No way. Dogs, cats, raccoons—those he could handle. Women like Mariah Brady were the kind of trouble he had learned the hard way to avoid.

Four

———

Mariah had learned a long time ago to stand on her own two feet. There was no earthly reason why she should start leaning now, just because she'd been presented with a pair of invitingly wide shoulders. After showering and blow-drying her hair, she dug out a pair of beige silk slacks that had cost an arm and a leg, even at a discount, and paired them with a baggy Peruvian sweater in shades of taupe, plum and malachite green.

It was still pouring down rain. The silk would water spot, but for reasons she didn't care to examine too closely, she put them on anyway. It couldn't rain forever.

Besides, when a woman looked her best, she rationalized as she smoothed her flyaway hair, she was better prepared to face whatever needed facing.

"Just as long as you remember that those inviting shoulders aren't yours to lean on." She puckered and touched her lips with a pale frosted tint. "All the man offered you is a lift and a temporary loan. Period."

She smoothed her eyebrows, picked up her mascara wand and put it back again. All mascara would do for eyes that were tired and shadowed from a lack of sleep was call attention to them.

Perhaps her dark glasses...

Then, snorting in disgust at the irrepressible romantic streak that she'd never quite managed to outgrow, she peeled off her finery, changed back into yesterday's jeans, rumpled her hair with her fingers, and scrubbed off her Desert Mirage lipstick.

Pride was such a silly thing. Underneath all her recently acquired posh and pizzazz she was still plain Sara Mariah Brady of the dishwater hair and the dishwater eyes—a shy, bespectacled beanpole who hadn't had a single date until she was almost twenty.

Reaching automatically for her purse, she remembered, swore, and let herself out the door. Gus was waiting outside—none too patiently, if his expression was anything to go by. He was wearing a fresh pair of rumpled khakis, these not quite so faded as yesterday's had been, topped with a white shirt and black leather bomber jacket. His hair looked at if it had been groomed with a hay rake. Shoulders braced, hands planted on his narrow hips, he scowled out at the dispirited drizzle.

"Good morning," she said with more cheerfulness than she felt.

He glared at her over his shoulder.

What now? she wondered, sighing. Last night they had parted as friends... acquaintances, at the very least. Or so she'd thought.

"Good morning, Gus," she repeated.

He shot her another nasty look, as though blaming her for the weather. "It took you long enough," he growled.

"It's seven twenty-three." Mariah looked pointedly at her watch. She'd been up since just past six, unable to sleep.

"I suppose you want breakfast before we check out."

She took a deep, steadying breath. If she'd been literally starving, she wouldn't have admitted it now. Forcing herself to smile, she replied that she could easily do without breakfast if he wanted to get on the road.

"Dammit, don't be so noble! Do you want breakfast or not?"

"Not." Wheeling back into her room, she began bringing out her bags, dumping them on the sheltered walkway outside her door. Using her one good hand, it was slow going, but she'd sooner turn green and die than ask for help.

With a low snarl, Gus brushed past her and shouldered her box of books. He jerked his head toward the truck. "Get in," he snapped.

"Get lost," she muttered under her breath. This, on top of a largely sleepless night and everything else, was just too much! Suddenly reversing her steps, she snatched her toilet case off the stack she had just deposited outside and marched back into the room.

"What the devil are you doing *now?*"

She turned and went back outside for her suitcase. "You're obviously in a hurry, so don't let me keep you. If you'll just bring my box back inside, please, I can get everything else and you can be on your way. Once I retrieve my car, I'll swing back by and collect my things." She spoke softly. Anyone who knew her well would have known to back off.

Gus didn't know her. "Don't be crazy. Get in the damned truck, Mariah."

"Go to the devil, Wydowski." Darn it, he was too pale to talk so tough. If he'd been hers to worry about, she would have been force-feeding him homemade soup by now, and making sure he got enough rest.

Well, he wasn't hers, thank the Lord for small favors.

As a shaft of watery sunshine tried to break through the clouds, Mariah noticed that he'd cut himself trying to trim his beard. She could have told him, if he'd bothered to ask, that it would take more than a trim to make him look even marginally civilized.

Smiling through clenched teeth, she said, "I believe I'll walk, thanks all the same." She would sooner poke her finger in a live socket than get in that truck with him again!

Without a word, he swept her up in his arms and one-handed the passenger door open. Talk about your short fuses! She tried to wriggle free. His arms tightened. She would have bopped him over the head with her good hand if she hadn't been afraid of landing flat on her keester in a puddle of dirty water.

As he thrust her inside the truck she tried to ignore the thousand or so volts of electricity that surged through her body wherever it came into contact with his. It was anger. Pure and simple anger. The dimmest wit would have better sense than to let herself be attracted to a man like Gus Wydowski.

Gus slammed the door shut and swung up into the driver's seat beside her. He rammed the key into the ignition, but instead of twisting it, he gripped the steering wheel and glared out through the windshield.

Was he counting to ten? Mariah devoutly hoped so. Her fondest wish was that she could irritate him as much as he irritated her.

"I asked you if you wanted some breakfast," he growled.

"No, you didn't. You insinuated—"

"I never insinuate. If I've got something to say, I damned well say it! Now, do you want breakfast first or not?"

She retaliated by becoming the grande dame, which was what Basil used to call her when she was trying her best to rise above a dismal situation. Crossing her legs at the ankles, she folded her hands in her lap, stretched her neck to its limit and composed her features. "If you don't mind, I'd rather you dropped me off at my car. I'd rather dine alone."

"Dine, my as—trophysics," he sneered. "Using what for money?"

If she'd had her purse she would have whacked him with it, grande dame or not. As it was, she had only one good hand left, and she didn't dare risk it. Not with a lively eight-month-old imp to look after. "Wydowski, did anyone ever tell you you make a lousy good samaritan?"

"Not that I recall."

"Then your memory must be every bit as rotten as your disposition."

She could almost have sworn she saw his lips twitch. Reluctantly she admitted that he had a nice mouth—firm without being hard. Which just went to show how deceptive appearances could be.

"We'll have breakfast first," he said, switching on the engine.

Oh, great. If she'd insisted on eating first, he would have driven her directly to her car and dumped her out. Now that they were about to part company, she was beginning to get the hang of handling him. *Don't eat all the carrots, Rosemary, save some for Burdy.* What did they call it—reverse psychology? It had worked with the kids.

Silently she vowed to write him a nasty little note to accompany the payment she intended to send him if she had to rob a bank to do it. The thought of having the last word brought a smug little smile to her lips.

At the crowded family style restaurant, Gus handed her a menu and waited. "No, thanks, I'm really not hungry." She should have waited in the truck, but he'd insisted she come with him, probably afraid she might jimmy the ignition and steal his blasted pickup.

A pink-uniformed waitress sashayed up to the table. Ignoring Mariah, she treated Gus to a toothy smile, which he returned with interest, Mariah noted sourly. He ordered the works: a full cholesterol special. Then he added, "Make it two, with a couple of side orders of pancakes." His gaze followed the friendly waitress as she swayed her way gracefully between tables. Then, turning back to Mariah, he said, "You need to eat something if you're going to make Muddy Whatsis today. Now, let's see you wiggle 'em for me."

"Wiggle *what* for you?"

The corner of his mouth twitched again. "Your fingers, honey. What did you think I meant?"

Gus had made a valiant effort to keep things on an impersonal level. Unfortunately, Mariah Brady was precisely the type of woman he'd always been a sucker for. The kind who could drag a burlap sack over her head, tie it at the waist with a rope, and look like a million bucks before taxes. There was only one trouble with these decorative types—they were all surface. About as deep as your average oil slick.

Although he had to admit that this one seemed to have a little more going for her than most of the beauties he'd been involved with in the past. Including Lisa.

Assistant manager of a feed and seed store? Was she putting him on? He could have sworn she was on the level, but it didn't add up. Not that feed and seed clerks couldn't wear fancy yellow britches and three-inch clogs, but he had a feeling she was leaving something out of her résumé. If there was one thing Gus couldn't abide, it was being played for a sucker.

Not that there was any chance of being played for anything, because he wasn't going to get involved, never mind the fact that all he'd been able to think about last night was getting her into his bed. Or himself into hers. He'd lain awake for hours after he'd gone to his own room, wondering what it would be like to kiss her. Wondering how it would feel to run his hands nice and slow and easy down that long, silken torso—to kiss his way down her throat and then taste those small, sweet breasts.

He'd wondered a lot more than that, too. Fortunately he had better sense than to try to satisfy his curiosity.

Making an effort to subdue his renegade libido, Gus told himself it was nothing personal. He'd always been a pushover when it came to ladies in need. Some guys never learned. That didn't mean he had to adopt them all, for crying out loud.

Realizing he'd been staring at the top button on her shirt, he shifted his gaze and said, "Well? Are you going to wiggle 'em, or not? I need to be sure all your parts are in working order before I let you go."

That got a rise out of her, all right. The lady wasn't quite as unflappable as she liked to pretend.

"Minor correction—you're not *letting* me go. I'm *going*," Mariah said sweetly.

"Yeah, sure. Now, wiggle your fingers for me, will you? I think the swelling's gone down some since last night."

It had. Her hand was no longer throbbing quite so much, but it was still swollen. The thought of bending her fingers made her wince. They were a nasty shade of purplish blue, the marks of the door clearly visible between the first and second joints of her ring

finger. Taking a deep breath, she wiggled them experimentally and couldn't quite suppress a sharp, indrawn breath.

"Not so good, huh?"

"Much better. The soreness is almost gone," she
lied.

The waitress brought their orders, and despite the
fact that she hadn't wanted anything, Mariah stared
hungrily at the mounds of scrambled eggs, bacon and
hash browns. Next to the plate of pancakes swim-
ming in syrup and butter, there was a basket of toast
and a plate of jelly, including a single tub of her favorite guava jam.

"Want me to feed you or can you manage a knife
and fork? Eating pancakes with your fingers is pretty
messy. Maybe you'd better tuck your napkin under
your chin, just in case you dribble." Gus grinned at
her. The man had a truly wicked smile.

"Do you enjoy humiliating people?"

Dumping his third packet of sugar into his coffee,
he cocked his head thoughtfully. "Yeah . . . now that
you mention it, I suppose I do. I used to enjoy the occasional spot of hunting, but blood sports take a lot of
energy. These days I usually settle for a round or two
of recreational humiliation. Doesn't require nearly as
much exertion."

"Beast," Mariah muttered. She grabbed the tub of
guava jam, set it beside her plate and stirred a sweet-
ener into her coffee, and then automatically lifted the
thick mug with her right hand.

Hot coffee splashed all down her front. She yelped
and grabbed her injured fingers with her left hand.

The mug rolled across the table and onto the floor just as Gus grabbed a fistful of napkins and started blotting her chest. What with the pain in her fingers and the sting of the hot coffee, it took several moments before she thought to shove his hand away from the front of her shirt.

Gus looked first stricken, then embarrassed. "Hey, I didn't mean—that is, I wasn't trying to—"

"I know." She did know, too. Gus might have more shortcomings than your average man, but she was pretty sure he wasn't the type to grope a lady in a crowded restaurant.

Or even in a motel room, late at night, when the rain and darkness enclosed them together into a small world of their own.

"Gus, it's all right, really." She plucked the clammy wet fabric away from her body. Oh, for goodness' sake, what a klutz she was! At this rate, everything she owned would be stained beyond redemption.

Ignoring her own vinyl slicker, Gus lifted his black leather jacket from the rack and draped it over her shoulders, and Mariah gathered it around her. The lingering warmth of his body felt good over her rapidly cooling wet shirt.

"Are you burned?"

"No, I don't think so. It wasn't all that hot."

"Maybe we'd better—"

"Gus, I'm all right—really! Although if I knew that much about astrology," she said with a despairing sort of chuckle, "I might be tempted to blame it on the stars. I think all mine must have gone on strike yesterday morning. What do they call it?"

"Call what?"

The waitress arrived with a towel and mopped up the river of coffee that dripped from the table onto the bench, and while Mariah worked her arms into the voluminous jacket and turned back the sleeves, Gus quietly requested a smaller, thinner cup.

"You know, when all the stars go backward?"

"I dunno. Apocalypse?"

"I'm beginning to believe it. It's called retro something. They're not really moving backward, it only looks that way, and it's supposed to cause all sorts of screwups. Burdy, one of my sisters, was into astrology last summer. She told me that my hardest years would be the earlier ones, but that things would look up after a while." She lifted her face and Gus tried his damnedest to ignore the deep shadows under her eyes and the hint of a quiver in her voice. "Is it after a while yet?"

He swore silently. It wasn't the shadows that got to him. It wasn't even the quiver. Dammit, it was that wistful little smile of hers that blew a hole a mile wide in his defenses. Scowling, he concentrated on cutting her pancakes, and they finished breakfast in silence.

Mariah thought that Gus was probably counting down the minutes, in spite of the fact that he was dawdling over his third cup of coffee, seemingly in no hurry to get on the road. Mariah told herself he was probably just taking one last stab at the good samaritan thing. She was beginning to feel guilty for some of the things she'd said to him. The poor guy couldn't help his disposition—it was probably genetic. In which case, if he came from a long line of grouchy people, he deserved sympathy.

"Look, in case I gave you the wrong impression, Gus, I really am grateful for everything you've done. You didn't have to help me at all. You could have left me at the convenience store and gone on your way to—well, to wherever it is you're going."

He shrugged. With another man, she might have thought he looked embarrassed. "Sunshine," he said. "Just looking for a little sunshine."

"Anyway, I just wanted you to know that I do appreciate everything you've done for me. I don't know what I would've done if—"

"You'd have done just fine," he growled.

"Yes, I would. I've been taking care of myself for nearly thirty years, but that doesn't mean— Oh, for heaven's sake, thank you! There, I've said it! You know, you really are a terrible grouch, Wydowski. I don't see how you can tolerate your own company."

At that, he grinned again, and she was struck once more by what a puzzling, exasperating—and yes, what a shockingly sexy man he was. Glowering at the slightly less-than-perfect white teeth and those penetrating eyes of his, Mariah gave up. Men like Gus Wydowski were totally outside her experience—and wasn't *that* a blessing! "Forget it, will you? I'm ready to go whenever you are," she said with a sigh, knowing even as she spoke that it was a lie.

Her car was still where she'd left it, intact so far as she could tell. Gus dealt with the clerk while Mariah dealt with her luggage, then she suffered the sharp edge of his tongue when he came out and caught her trying to juggle the heavy box of books with two arms and one good hand.

"You're nuts, you know that? You're not safe to be out in the world on your own." He lifted the box from her arms and dumped it into her back seat. "Your tires are practically bald. Do you have a spare?"

"Certainly I have a spare, it's in the trunk along with the tools."

"Let's see your key, I'd better check it out just in case."

She had the one key she had stashed under the hood. It fit the ignition, not the trunk. She told him so, and then listened while he unraveled a few more yards of profanity. It occurred to her even as she waited for him to get it out of his system that there were different types of profanity. Gus's was angry, but it wasn't smutty. Smut offended her, but anger she understood.

"If you've finished with your damning and helling, I'd like to be on my way."

"Let me see you start her and back her around."

"Wha-a-at?"

"Mariah, if you can't grip a steering wheel and change gears, how the devil do you plan to make it all the way to Muddy Whatsis?"

"Landing! It's Muddy Landing!" If she sounded upset, it was only because she'd been wondering the same thing. If she couldn't even hold a heavy coffee mug, how was she going to get herself home? And even if she did, how on earth was she ever going to handle twenty-odd pounds of active, squirming, little girl?

"Have you decided which way you're going? There's a lot of traffic on I-95, but I'm not sure the other route's much better."

"I'll manage just fine. And now, I really do have to go. Gus, thank you again. For everything. I'll send you a check just as soon as I—"

He cut her off in a way that left her reeling on her feet. Catching her by her shoulders, he hauled her up against him, taking care not to touch her right hand, and kissed her. It was no friendly little peck, either. His mouth was hard and warm and thorough. He tasted of coffee, and to her amazement Mariah found that she wanted to touch him all over, to hold him with both arms and not let go.

A moment later, staring at his dark, scowling face as he swung up into his truck, she remembered to close her mouth.

"Well...damn," she whispered.

Gus headed south. Mariah watched until his taillights disappeared in the misty rain. A few minutes later she was headed north, furious for no real reason at all. She had a full tank of gas; she was within a few hours of home, and she was managing without an unbearable amount of discomfort in spite of the fact that everything except for the turn signal, which she hardly needed on the interstate, required the use of her right hand.

"Damn the man, anyway," she muttered as she stopped at a traffic light just outside Jacksonville. She fancied she could still taste his kiss. She had never been kissed by a bearded man before, and she couldn't decide whether she'd liked it or not.

Oh, she'd liked it, all right. Heavens, yes, she'd liked it! Even more, she had liked the feel of his hard body against hers, the leathery, soapy, masculine scent of him and the feel of those arms holding her so close she could hardly breathe—arms that could offer shelter, protection and goodness knows what else to some lucky woman.

By the time she got through Jacksonville, she was still going over it in her mind. It was a good thing, she decided, that he'd gone his way and she'd gone hers, because the last thing she needed in her life at this point was another complication.

And Gus Wydowski would be a complication of the most complicated sort!

Five

Gus made it as far south as Jupiter Beach. The rain had stopped, but it was still untropically cold. Not exactly beach-lying, bone-baking weather. He considered heading on down to the Keys. He still had time. There was nothing to stop him. No reason why he couldn't go wherever he took a notion to go and stay as long as he wanted to stay, just so long as he got back in time to get started on the Paragon Shores project on schedule.

So how come he was headed north again?

He didn't even want to know. One thing he did know: it had nothing to do with the woman. He had no intention of going anywhere near Muddy What-sis—if such a place even existed. Probably one of these little backwoods swamp settlements where everyone was kin to everyone else—sometimes a little too close kin for comfort.

On the other hand, it might not have occurred to her that along with everything else, the creeps who had snatched her purse had access to her address as well as her house keys. They'd headed south, sure, but the highway ran both ways.

Gus told himself there was little chance they would follow her home. If she'd had a St. Augustine address, there might have been a danger, but no two-bit hoods were going to follow a mark all the way to Georgia on the off chance that she had something at home worth stealing.

Still, as long as he was passing through the neighborhood, it wouldn't hurt to make sure she was all right. It didn't mean he had any personal interest. He would have done the same for anyone under similar circumstances. Jeez, a guy would have to be a big-time loser to get involved with a woman like that just because she happened to appeal to him physically.

Right. And food appealed to a starving man.

Absently he scratched his jaw as a slow grin spread over his face. Man, would she evermore be ticked off if he were to show up on her doorstep. Might even be worth going a couple of miles out of his way just to see the look on her face.

Gus had no illusions about his own attractions. He had a healthy bank account, which made up for a number of shortcomings, but even so, he was no great prize. He'd been called a lot of things by a lot of women: a battle-scarred, pig-headed loner with a lousy disposition being among the milder descriptions. And that didn't even take into account the addiction he was doing his damnedest to kick.

Namely, women. Women like Mariah. Women who might be spoiled and superficial, but who were so damned good to look at, a man clean forgot to check under the hood until it was too late.

He was beginning to think Mariah might be different, but then, he'd been fooled before. If he was smart, he'd detour around by way of Tennessee instead of deliberately riding into an ambush.

On the other hand, he thought a few miles later as he popped a handful of M&M's, Mariah had mentioned the fact that Muddy Whatsis was only a mile or two off Highway 17. He'd be passing right by the place. It would be downright discourteous not to swing past just to make sure she'd got home all right. Five minutes tops, and he'd be on his way north again. In a day or so, he'd have forgotten all about that wistful little smile of hers and her husky little laugh.

Not to mention a few other assets.

Spotting a smoky half a mile ahead, Gus eased up on the gas pedal. The last thing he needed at this point was to get involved with the Georgia highway patrol.

Or, for that matter, with the princess of Muddy Whatsis.

Mariah put the dishes in to soak and tuned the radio to a rock station. She hated it, but Jessie seemed to like it, judging by the way she chortled and bobbed up and down, hanging on to the playpen rail with one wet fist, waving the other to keep time.

Even teething—even away from home, with an aunt she hardly knew, Jessie was a happy baby. Mariah didn't know how she would have coped if her niece had been any less laid back. She'd got home Friday night, too exhausted to unpack, fallen into bed and slept for nine hours straight. Basil and Jessie had arrived early Saturday morning. Basil had been in such a rush to get off again that he hadn't even asked how she'd hurt her hand, much less if it was going to be a problem.

Poor Basil. It was not that he was insensitive, he just had a lot on his mind, what with Myrtiss taking off like that and having to leave his business in the hands of a high school boy while he brought Jessie here and then go racing off in search of his wife. He had checked with her parents in Arkansas, but if Myrtiss was there, they weren't saying so. He'd just have to go and see.

Mariah had tried to absorb all the information about vitamins and which foods went with which meals, and about keeping small nonedibles out of reach.

She had learned right off that everything was edible, and that nothing within reach of those greedy little fists was safe. Jessie couldn't walk yet, but one way or another she covered ground remarkably fast, pulling herself up on everything. Mariah had spent that first morning trying to keep up with her and childproof the house at the same time. As far as she knew, she'd succeeded, thanks to the folding playpen Basil had remembered to bring along.

And finally, thank goodness, the sun had decided to shine again! Except for the water standing in the low sections of her yard—which was just about everywhere—you wouldn't even know it had rained for a solid week. As soon as things dried up a little more, Mariah intended to drag the playpen out onto the porch so she could work outside. She'd neglected her yard for too long.

The althaeas, for instance, weren't happy by the back fence. She thought the soil might be too sour. Maybe if she moved them over near the azaleas she had transplanted last year...

But then, her azaleas hadn't grown an inch, either. In fact, if she didn't soon see a little improvement, she was going to dig up every last one and move them to a new location.

That is, she would once she could handle a shovel again. So far, she could barely manage a broom. Driving all the way home hadn't helped her hand any.

"Jessie, spit that out!" Kneeling beside the playpen, Mariah tried to pry what looked like a shoestring from her niece's mouth. "Sweetie, you can't be hungry so soon," she muttered. "You've already eaten toast and a bowlful of gluck—what didn't end up on the floor or the walls, at least."

The baby clamped her four teeth together, openly delighting in the game. Mariah had learned two things about her niece in the short time they'd been together, the first being that whatever came within reach of Jessie's pudgy little fists ended up in Jessie's mouth.

The second being that babies were slippery when wet. Which was far more often than one would imagine.

Over the noise of the radio, Mariah didn't hear the sound of the truck pulling up in her front yard. Not until Jessie glanced over her shoulder and beamed that wet, snaggle-toothed smile of hers did she even glance around.

Her eyes widened. "Oh, my... Gus? What on earth are you doing here? I've got the check all ready to mail to your home address as soon as I can get to the post office for a stamp."

"Is it supposed to be eating string?"

"Is *what* supposed to be—" Tearing her eyes away from the last man she'd ever expected to see again, Mariah turned back to Jessie. "Honey, spit it out. Come on now, give the string to Aunt Ri."

Clasping her by the shoulders, Gus shifted Mariah to one side and took over as if he'd been dealing with such crises forever. "You heard the lady, spit it out, kid. You get that thing tangled around those pearly nubs of yours and you're going to be gumming your grits and greens from now on." Deftly, he removed the soggy bit of frayed plastic tape from Jessie's mouth and handed it to Mariah.

"It must have come off her playpen pad. She eats everything she gets her hands on. Right now, she's real partial to chair rungs, but I thought she was safe in her pen." Mariah tried to force her heart to slow down. He was back! She'd told herself she had seen the last of him, and almost succeeded in convincing herself that she didn't care. "Gus, what on earth are you doing here? I thought you were headed for the beach."

What he was doing was rubbing noses with Jessie, to the baby's noisy delight. "You mean, what am I doing besides falling in love?"

Mariah felt as if she'd just stepped off the edge of the earth. "In... love?" she whispered. It was too soon. He couldn't...

"What's her name? Does she always take to strangers this way?"

Jessie, in pink corduroy overalls, with a pink ribbon dangling from her few stands of sandy hair, was beaming at Gus. Gus was beaming right back. Mariah's heart settled back into place with a dull thud. "Her name is Jessica Brady, and no, she doesn't always take to strangers right off. Maybe you remind her of Butch."

"Butch?"

"Myrtiss's Yorkshire terrier." It was a snide remark, but she made it anyway. She owed him something for showing up this way, just when she was planning to start putting him out of her mind any day now.

"Can I— I mean, what if I tried to pick her up? Would she let me? Is there a special way to do it?"

"Oh, Jessie'll let anyone pick her up. The trouble comes when you try to put her down again."

Gus obviously wasn't worrying about the future. "What do I do first?"

Mariah closed her eyes and tried to ignore the warm, melting feeling spreading rapidly inside her. Drat the man! Why did he have to look so tough on the outside when he was nothing but a marshmallow on the inside? How could a woman fight against a man like that? "Stand up and hold out both hands." She showed him how. "She'll do the rest."

Gus had taken one look at the blue-eyed, fat-cheeked, bow-legged mite in baggy pink overalls, and turned to mush. "She sure puts a hell of a...a heck of a lot of body English into that smile of hers, doesn't she?" Maybe this uncle business wasn't going to so bad after all, if Alex and Angel had something like this.

He held out his hands and waited, and sure enough, Jessie did her part. Turning loose the railing, she stood for an instant on chubby, wobbly feet—one sock on, one off—and lifted her hands.

"Tay, tay," she chortled.

Worried, Gus glanced at Mariah. "What's she saying?"

"Take, take. Lift her up under her arms and then hang on—she wiggles like an earthworm. If she takes a notion she wants to come to Aunt Ri—that's me," Mariah said self-consciously, "she'll lunge, ready or not."

Gus's big hands encompassed the small torso. Cautiously he lifted the beaming baby and settled her in his arms. She was sort of like a puppy, only she smelled sweeter. And no pup ever had a smile like that!

He grinned proudly as Jessie discovered his beard and began tugging with both hands.

"She's playing horsey," Mariah said dryly.

"Glad she's not wearing spurs." He enclosed one tiny foot in his hand, a look of sheer enchantment on his face.

A few hours later Gus sat at the kitchen table watching Jessie shovel food into her mouth with both hands. "You know, you were right—she's eaten everything on her plate," he said proudly.

"Except for what's on the floor, the tray and her clothes, not to mention yours."

"When's she going to get some hair?"

"She has hair, it's just sort of transparent. That's why I tied a ribbon on the few strands she has. They're brown, by the way."

"Oh. I thought that brown stuff was food. How about teeth? Will she get any more?"

"She's working on it. Gus, don't you know anything at all about babies?"

"Nope. Know something about kids—boys, that is. Couple of men in my construction crew have boys old enough to want to hang around the site, but nobody I know ever had a baby."

Mariah felt herself sinking deeper. No man could be all that guileless. "I expect even boys are babies at one stage in their lives."

"I never thought much about it. Hey, look at that, she's doing it again! Do all babies smile this way?"

"What way?" Mariah was busy putting the finishing touches on supper. Gus had made a run on the grocery store, bringing back T-bone steaks, ice cream, cookies, store-bought cake and pounds of bananas. Jessie loved bananas.

"Like, all the time?"

The steaks were done to perfection. Mariah didn't like any pink showing. "She's a particularly happy baby. She's always been that way. Not all of them are." Rosemary had been colicky. Mariah barely remembered Alethia, Burdy and Basil as babies, she'd been so young at the time, but she didn't recall a whole lot of smiling. Mostly she remembered hanging endless diapers on the line, hearing Daddy fuss about money and Mama's "sickness," and being told to keep those young'uns quiet or he'd go cut a switch and do the job himself.

"Here, I hope you like your steak well done," she said. She'd cooked rice because she had some in the pantry, but there hadn't been time to cook collards, which was all that was left of her garden. "Sorry about the lack of vegetables. I haven't had a chance to go shopping because Basil went off with Jessie's car seat."

"No problem. Rice is a vegetable, isn't it?"

Gus made a mental note to go buy a baby seat for her car before he left. He didn't want to go off and leave her here with no way to get around. "By the way, have you done anything about replacing your driver's license?"

"I've hardly had time yet."

"How are you going to haul Jessie around without a basket or something? You don't want to break too many laws at once."

"I'll deal with it," she said sharply, and Gus lifted his eyebrows. The lady was touchy. Her hand must be hurting her more than she wanted to admit.

Refusing his offer of help, she plopped his plate down in front of him with her left hand. He noted the curling edges of his T-bone and sighed. She did know how to ruin a perfectly good piece of beef, he thought with a sigh. But at least she tried. Lisa couldn't boil water and was proud of the fact. Actually, the rice looked pretty good. If you liked rice. He didn't.

Gus insisted on washing dishes. The place didn't run to a dishwasher. From what he'd seen so far, it didn't run to much else except termites, damp rot and old age. Even the plumbing had emphysema. It was big. Fifty years ago it might have been a decent house, but about all it was good for now was dozer fodder. The floor sloped. The roof sagged like a hammock. There wasn't a plumb line in the entire house, what with the foundation, such as it was, having settled into the ground over the last half century.

The inside was marginally better. The walls were painted yellow. There were curtains at the windows, but they were tied up out of reach of small hands. The furniture with its cheerful, faded slipcovers, looked comfortable, if well used. There was a lineup of framed photos on the wall, and Gus had already been introduced to Rosemary, who proudly wore a student nurse's cap, to Alethia, who had her sister's cheekbones, to Burdina, who hadn't, and to Basil, who looked like a nerd. An earnest one, but still a nerd.

He'd mentioned the fact that all the end tables and coffee tables were bare. There was a box of books still waiting to be unpacked. Lamps, vases and other odds and ends were piled on every surface above waist high, which seemed a bit peculiar—he'd wondered out loud if the nearby river rose all that high.

"It's Jessie. She eats everything she gets her hands on, and she can get her hands on more than you'd ever believe."

Gus thought now about the house. He thought about the baby. He thought about his own building projects. What he tried hard not to think about was Mariah. Walking in and seeing her like that, bending over that baby coop thing with her yellow sweats clinging to her hips and her hair slipping in wisps from under the scarf she'd tied around her head—it had hit him even harder than the flu bug had.

Ever since he'd driven off and left her at that dinky little convenience store, the taste of her still on his tongue, the smell of lilac lingering in his memory like the promise of spring, he'd done his best to convince himself that she was just one more attractive woman in a world full of attractive women. Most of 'em had enough going for them to keep a man interested for a few days—at most, a few months. Few of them, however, had that certain something that reached right inside a man and got him so snarled up he lost sight of all common sense.

Gus told himself it was time to move on. No way was he going to get involved with the hard-luck queen of nowheresville, just because she happened to be the kind of a woman who could drape herself in a plastic drop cloth and outclass every other woman in the state of Georgia.

A couple more hours. A couple more hours, he promised himself, and he'd hit the road. There was plenty of light left, even after the last dish was washed. Not quite the end of February, but already the days were getting longer.

Rack up another winter, Gus thought, feeling oddly restless. While Mariah finished putting away the dishes, he entertained the baby, who showed no signs of being sleepy. "She hates to give up," said Mariah. "Don't you, puss? So much to chew, so little time."

Raking back his kitchen chair, Gus suggested they go outside for a breather. "Jessie wants to work a few kinks out, she's been penned up too long, haven't you, possum?"

Mariah glanced at him, and then glanced quickly at the red teapot-shaped clock. Was that some subtle hint, as if she was afraid he might try to move in on her? "Don't worry, I'll be hitting the road in a few minutes," he reassured her. "I just thought as long as I was in the neighborhood, I might as well stop off and see that you made it home all right."

Jessie started bouncing her padded little bottom on his arm, and he secured her so that she could bounce and not fall. Amazing, how fast a guy picked up these things. Apparently he had talents he hadn't even discovered yet.

"You didn't have to stop, Gus, but thanks. It was right thoughtful of you." Mariah switched off the light over the sink and headed for the back door, and Gus followed with Jessie, his gaze on the woman in the yellow sweats. She hadn't taken time to change for dinner... but then, neither had he.

Thoughtful of him? Sure it was. Just like he didn't have a thought in his head that wasn't pure as driven snow. *Wydowski, you're a real bastard, you know that?*

He liked the way she moved. Sort of stiff-legged, awkward and graceful all at the same time. He wondered what she would look like without those baggy sweats. Without anything at all.

Jessie was babbling something as she tugged on his beard, so he missed most of what Mariah was saying as she plucked a leaf and crumbled it in her left hand. "Didn't bloom last year, so I moved them to where they'd get a little more sunlight. But even so. . ."

He was picturing her in a low-cut, slinky gown with rhinestone straps. Something short. With mile-high heels and stockings with those webby little things embroidered all over them. He could see her sipping champagne and laughing at some guy in a tux. A good-looking, clean-shaven guy who— "Whoa. You don't want to eat that, honey," he said as Jessie leaned in and took a bite of his beard.

"Let me take her. You're bound to be tired after driving all day." Mariah brushed the crumbled leaves off her shirt and held out her arms. Gus found himself wishing with all his heart she would hold out her arms to him.

Down boy. "She's okay, just still hungry, I guess. Better let me hang on to her, she's feeling frisky and you've still got that bum hand."

Besides, as long as he had an armful of Jessie, he couldn't get into too much trouble with her Aunt Ri.

Mariah felt as if she'd had too much wine, too fast, on an empty stomach. She wanted him to go, but she wanted even more for him to stay. She couldn't look at him without remembering the way they'd parted.

Had he forgotten?

Did he kiss all the women he spent the night with that way?

Would he kiss her goodbye when he left this time, too?

Lord ha' mercy, she hoped not! She'd probably lean just a moment too long against that strong, hard body and he'd get all sorts of wrong ideas, and...

Embarrassed, Mariah concentrated on not looking at Gus. Instead she scowled at the house that was semisilhouetted against a coral sky. Along the long, potholed driveway, a handful of tall Georgia pines stood out like gaunt sentinels. Moss hung from a huge cypress tree just outside the property line—she'd always loved that tree. Basil said it was a good thing it was too big to dig up, else she'd have brought it home with her long before now.

Gus stood beside her and looked at the house, too, trying to think of something tactful to say. It was a real mess. An unpainted, run-down house in the middle of the flattest, wettest, most dismal country he'd ever seen outside the Everglades. The only decent thing about it was the yard, and even that was...

Well, it was weird, was what it was. Gus knew something about landscaping. His sister owned a landscape nursery in Durham. This place could serve as the before part of a before-and-after picture, with its concrete menagerie, its hanging gourds and half a dozen or so birdbaths, all chipped or jury-rigged in some fashion or another. There were plastic milk cartons suspended by a length of clothesline over a few of them, dripping water into the overflowing bowls.

And then there was the shrubbery. He recognized a few specimens from being around Angel's place. All he could say was whoever did this job must have had one hell of an astigmatism.

"Is that thing supposed to be a deer or a horse?" he asked.

"It's mostly deer. Grover sold yard sculpture, and I got the seconds and broken pieces free for hauling them off. The kids put this one together from odd parts. His name is Eugene. He was their favorite," Mariah said somewhat defensively.

"What happened to this section of yard? It's all chopped up, but nothing's growing there."

"I'm not finished yet. I've been away since last summer."

They were strolling around the house, Gus entertaining Jessie while Mariah commented idly about this plant and that one. Suddenly the whole scenario reminded him a little too much of couples he'd seen strolling around, admiring their houses while they were still under construction.

Sweet salvation, he had to get out of here! "Hey, look, this is nice, but I'd better be hitting the road," he said, prying Jessie's fingers from his beard. In the shadowy light it was almost possible to convince himself that was disappointment he saw on her face.

"So soon? But you just got here. I know you must be eager to get home, but, Gus, I've got plenty of room," Mariah heard herself saying. "It's getting late.

You'd have to put up somewhere, anyway, unless you plan to drive on through tonight.''

"I don't mind a little night driving—less traffic. Anyway, you don't need another houseguest, you've got both hands full with this little sky diver.'' Gus made a swift correction in his grip as Jessie lunged unexpectedly. She was getting fretful. "On the other hand,'' he suggested, "I could help you get her settled for the night. After that, I might enjoy one last cup of coffee before I hit the road.''

"Fine,'' Mariah said proudly. She refused to beg. If he couldn't see how much she wanted him to stay, how much she needed him, then let him go. "I guess I could use some help with Jessie's bath,'' she said. "She really is slippery when she's wet and soapy.''

Six

Every instinct told Gus to get out while he still could. The more he was around her, the more he was beginning to suspect that Mariah Brady was a permanent sort of woman. In which case, the last thing she needed was a temporary guy like him messing up her life.

Sure, she turned him on. When it came to class, she was in a class by herself, but that was only a part of the problem. Classy looks, a sense of humor—add to that the fact that she was a real nice lady?

Uh-uh. No way. It was too risky a proposition for any man whose immunity was showing cracks the size of the Grand Canyon.

They stood in the doorway of the small bedroom, gazing at the clean, sleepy baby in the battered old crib

Mariah had dragged down from the attic. Jessie offered them a wet smile and made baby noises.

"What's she saying?" Gus asked.

"She's saying, thanks for not dropping me while you were getting me ready for bed, Aunt Ri."

Without thinking, Gus draped a companionable arm over her shoulder, and then wished he hadn't. "How can you be so sure?"

"It's instinct. Women just know these things, that's all." She grinned as she said it, and Gus felt a few more symptoms kick in. Touching her was a mistake. He cleared his throat and began to ease away, hoping she didn't notice he was having trouble with his breathing again. If she did, maybe she'd put it down to his cough, even though he hadn't coughed in a couple of days.

Mariah noticed. She noticed everything about him, much to her regret. The heat and weight of his arm. Those iron-hard muscles in his forearms where his sleeves were turned back. The thick dusting of dark curly hair that made her wonder if he was hairy all over.

Hairy men had never appealed to her until now. Until Gus. He was so shaggy, so sweet—so tough and yet so tender. She was sadly afraid her taste in men had undergone an irreversible change.

He cleared his throat, and she reminded herself that he'd recently been sick. Was it depraved to lust after a man who was still suffering from the aftermath of the flu?

"How's the cough?" she asked. At least she could take care of his health, even if she couldn't take care of anything else.

Gus cleared his throat experimentally. "Better. Thanks."

"Have you had any more coughing spells?"

"A few. Not many. None lately."

He stepped back, casually disengaging his arm, and Mariah resisted a powerful urge to grab him and hang on. "This year's flu seems to hang on a lot longer than usual. I know of one woman who went back to work too soon and ended up having a relapse and having to be hospitalized."

"Hmm," Gus murmured. He was in danger, all right, but it wasn't from any flu bug. How the hell could a woman look so fine and smell so sweet in a pair of baggy sweats she'd been wearing all day?

Closing his eyes, he breathed in the essence of baby powder, steak and lilacs, a perfume that could make a fortune for anyone smart enough to bottle and market it.

"She's sound asleep already, bless her little heart," Mariah whispered. "Come on back to the kitchen while I make a pot of fresh coffee."

One for the road, to keep him alert, that was only being smart, right? One cup and he'd get out of here while he still could. Tomorrow, as soon as the stores opened, he would call around and have a car seat delivered. Maybe a big new teddy bear. Maybe even a dozen or so roses, because a woman like Mariah deserved roses. Or maybe orchids—although he wasn't sure there was a florist within delivering distance from

Muddy Whatsis that could handle a big order of orchids.

Still, the idea appealed to him. He didn't know what the devil she'd been doing down in Florida, but any lady who had grown up in a dump like this deserved a big bunch of orchids at least once in her life.

The coffeemaker burbled cheerfully while Mariah got out the mugs, the creamer, and refilled the sugar bowl. Gus watched her, liking the unselfconscious way she moved. Liking everything about her.

Liking it a little too much.

When the coffee was ready she poured with her good hand, handed him his, and he added three heaping spoonfuls of sugar, wondering what she would think when she opened the door to see a jungle-size arrangement of orchids. It would almost be worth hanging around long enough to watch.

No, it wouldn't. "Mariah, you might want to have someone check out those front steps before too long. You've got an accident waiting to happen there. Next thing you know, you'll have a lawsuit on your hands."

"The middle step. I meant to have it fixed before I left last summer, but there's only one odd-jobs man around these parts, and his arthritis was bothering him."

They were seated across the table from each other, talking about mundane things like rotten boards, sipping coffee and nibbling the dry, store-bought cake Gus had provided. Neither of them was thinking about broken steps, or even coffee and cake.

Mariah was thinking, How can I make him stay? It's no good unless he wants to stay, and why should he want to do that?

She might as well have thrown away her contacts and her fancy, custom-blended makeup. The closer she'd got to home, the more that shy, gawky, bean-pole self-image she'd carried around for so long had crept back, until it completely overshadowed her brief life as the glamorous, desirable, enigmatic Mariah.

The enigmatic part had been Vic's idea. "Dollface, if we're going to build you into this fabulous creature, you're going to have to keep your mouth shut until you learn to fake a decent accent. No designer in his right mind would dream of showing off his creations on some rube from Hicksville." Tact had never been Vic's strong suit.

Absently, Gus watched as she licked sugary frosting off her thumb, then wiped her hands on her yellow sweatshirt. Pity she didn't qualify for the swimsuit edition of that sports magazine.

32-A, he mused. 34-A, at the most. He wondered if she was self-conscious about being so small and hoped not. Angel used to stuff cotton in her bra until he told her once that if she couldn't balance the load any better, there was no point in wasting all that cotton. His kid sister was short, broad in the beam, and flat as a pancake—not that he'd heard any complaints from her husband, who happened to be Gus's best friend.

Mariah, on the other hand, was perfectly proportioned. Gus had an eye for such things, having once studied architecture. If he'd had the designing of her body himself, there wasn't one single part he would change.

Which, in itself, was pretty damn scary. "Look, this is nice, but I really need to get going. If I leave right now, I can make Savannah in time to get a few hours of sleep."

The refrigerator cut on. A funny-looking clock ticked noisily. The old house creaked as it settled a little deeper in the primordial mud of east Georgia. As a trysting place, it was about as unromantic as it could get. Laughable, in fact.

So how come he was thinking about orchids and roses and bosoms? How come was he so turned on he was embarrassed to get up from the table?

Gus felt his face grow warm about the same time that he felt the tickle in his throat. He tried to suppress the cough and nearly strangled, and Mariah jumped up and started whacking him on the back.

Talk about romantic. "I'm okay," he gasped when he could speak again. "Piece of cake went down the wrong way."

"Gus, you're not leaving here in this condition."

He glared at her, not trusting himself to speak.

"Look, I didn't ask you to follow me home," she said earnestly. "That was your choice. But you're pale and exhausted, certainly not fit to be out on the highway, and I refuse to have your death on my conscience."

Helpless to argue at the moment, Gus watched an increasingly familiar look of determination settle over her features. "Oh, yeah?" he managed.

She planted her hands on her hips, drawing the soft fabric taut across her flat abdomen until the faint shadow of a belly button appeared. Which didn't do much to improve his condition. "Gus, you know good and well you don't really want to drive any farther tonight, now, do you?"

He knew what he wanted to do, all right, and it had nothing to do with driving. But he didn't figure she was ready to hear what it was he really wanted. "I don't want to put you to any trouble," he rasped.

"Fine. Then see that you don't. If it'll make you feel any better, I'll tell you where the linen closet is and point you in the direction of a bed, and you can take it from there."

Gus knew when he was outmatched. When it came to stubborn, the lady could give lessons to a mule. How else had she been able to drive herself home and take care of a baby with a hand that must still be giving her a lot of grief?

"Thanks, Aunt Ri," he said with a reluctant grin. "I guess it wouldn't hurt to lay over one night. I can make up for lost time tomorrow."

"You're so gracious," she snapped. She marched out of the kitchen and returned a moment later, plopping a windup alarm clock on the table in front of him. "Set it as early as you like. Help yourself to breakfast, shut the door on your way out, and bon voyage!"

Oboy. Now he'd made her mad. "Look, Mariah, speaking of doors—"

"And try not to wake Jessie when you leave."

"Dammit, woman—"

"I'll thank you not to swear in my house. It sets a bad example for the baby."

"She's not even here!" he all but shouted, and she shushed him fiercely.

"Come on, I'll show you where everything is."

He clumped along behind her, the soles of his boots gritting on the worn hardwood floors. Miss High and Mighty! Her Royal Highness, Queen Mariah of Muddy Landing! He'd like to show *her* where everything was—and what to do with it!

Gus was asleep almost as soon as his head hit the pillow. The pillow that, along with all the bedding, had a damp and slightly musty smell, as if they'd been shut up in a closed house for a long time. But the bed was comfortable, and he was more tired than he wanted to admit. Chasing an elusive sun could downright frazzle a man to pieces.

Sometime during the night he came awake, shrouded by silence and darkness. It took several moments to get his bearings, and once he did, he lay there for several minutes wondering what had awakened him—adjusting himself to the subtle noises of an unfamiliar house.

The toilet. The damned commode was running! He didn't know if she had a well or municipal water— probably a well, because he hadn't seen anything faintly resembling a municipality.

Besides, unless he was very much mistaken, that was the hum of a well pump he was hearing in the background.

With a soft, sleepy oath, he swung his legs out of bed, raked a hand through his hair and stood up. Cool night air struck his naked body, bringing him sharply awake. He might as well shut the thing off before it sucked her well dry and burned up her pump.

Getting dressed first never occurred to him. There was no light showing, no sign that anyone else in the house was awake. He'd just shut off the valve and maybe take a look under the lid before he headed north in the morning. It was the least he could do in exchange for his night's lodging.

Having left his flashlight in the truck, Gus felt his way along the hall. He had almost reached the bathroom door when his hand collided with something soft and warm where nothing soft and warm should be.

"Jeez!" He jerked back his hand.

"Who? Gus?"

"Mariah? What are you doing, wandering around in the dark?"

"The commode's running. It sticks sometimes if you don't jiggle the handle just right. Go back to bed, I'll fix it."

"I might as well take a look, as long as I'm up."

He could feel the heat of her body reaching out to him, smell the scent of lilac and warm, clean woman. It was a lethal combination.

"Let me get the light," she said, just as he remembered his state of undress.

"Wait! Don't switch it on!"

"Why on earth not? Gus, go back to bed."

"Just don't turn on a light, that's all." He sensed her movement and reached out to stop her from embarrassing them both. His hand encountered a towel, and he snatched it down and tied it around his waist.

The sound of a handle being jiggled was clearly identified. Next he heard the sound of running water change pitch as the tank began to fill. "I'll check it out in the morning," he said, feeling at a distinct disadvantage.

"Don't bother, I wouldn't want to hold you up. Moe Chitty can take a look at it when he gets time."

"You want to pay a plumber, I guess that's your business."

"Moe's not a plumber. He's an auto mechanic, but he can fix anything and he doesn't charge much."

Already Gus didn't like the sound of Moe Chitty. Probably some smooth-talking type who'd resort to anything to get into her knickers. He started to say so when they both heard the baby whimper. They froze. It didn't occur to either of them that there was something slightly ludicrous about standing in a pitch-dark bathroom in the middle of the night, arguing about plumbing.

"Shh," said Mariah. "I don't think she's actually awake, but Basil said if she hears voices, she'll want to play all night."

"Sounds pretty good to me."

"You've got to be joking."

"Yeah ... I'm just joking." They were still whispering, standing closer now so that they could talk without rousing the baby. Gus had never been more serious in his life, only it was Mariah he wanted to play with, not her niece. He'd fallen hard for the little charmer, but it was the big charmer he was more interested in at the moment. Standing here beside her in the darkness, all he could think about was what it would be like to lay her down and make sweet, slow love to her all night long.

And then wake up and do it again and again, until neither one of them had the strength to crawl out of bed.

"Mariah..." he whispered hoarsely, reaching out just as she did.

What happened next was inevitable. Just before the last glimmer of reason disappeared and animal instinct took over, Gus told himself they'd been building up to this ever since she'd barged through the door of that dinky little convenience store down in Florida and practically tumbled right into his arms.

"Oh, Gus, I don't think this is very smart."

"Hush. We'll worry about it later if you want to."

It was a good thing he'd grabbed that towel, Gus told himself, because he didn't know her well enough yet to be kissing her while one of them was jaybird naked. He might not have a college degree, but Gus had his own sense of fairness, and unilateral nudity wasn't fair unless both parties knew about it.

He found her mouth in the darkness. It was incredibly sweet, oddly familiar—*right*. Everything about her was right—the taste of her, the way her lips trembled for a split second before they conformed to his own. The way she fit in his arms, her pelvic bone pushing against his groin, her breasts mashed against his chest. She couldn't have fit him more perfectly, he thought, as if she'd been created to his specifications. It was like coming home. Closing his eyes in the darkness, he heard the sound of a muffled groan and wondered fleetingly whose throat it had come from—hers or his.

Restlessly, Mariah wrapped her arms around his neck, wanting desperately to touch him everywhere at once. He was so hard, so hot. His body felt positively feverish! She ran her hands down his back, startled to discover that he wasn't wearing a pajama top.

The tip of his tongue pushed against hers—just the tip. He used it skillfully, like a saber, not a battering ram. Carefully he traced the line between her lips, nibbled little kisses, grazing her with his teeth and then soothing her with his tongue, his beard adding an unbearable degree of excitement to it all.

When she felt his palm cover her breast, she sagged against him, her breath catching in her throat as lightning streaked through her, leaving glowing, throbbing coals wherever it touched.

Alive in every cell of her body, she felt his muscles flex as he shifted position, felt him thrust powerfully against her belly. She was wearing a thin cotton nightshirt, but it might as well have been nothing at all.

His mouth lifted, and she could have wept, but then she felt his teeth graze her throat, felt his tongue on the small hollow at the base of her throat. How could she have lived this long without realizing what an exquisitely sensitive spot that was?

Her legs trembled with the urge to spread. As if sensing her surrender, Gus pushed his thigh between hers, and she felt his burning heat reach out to her in waves, felt the incredibly exciting roughness of his hairy thigh against her smooth one.

She slid her hands down his back to his waist, then moved them lower, cupping his taut masculine buttocks. A bit of coarse fabric slithered to the floor. His skin was like cool silk.

"Gus?" she murmured, startled.

"Shh, don't wake the baby." The movement of his lips caused his beard to brush against her neck, even as his thumbs toyed with her achingly sensitive nipples.

"Gus, what were you wearing?"

His voice sounded as if it were strained through burlap. "Not much," he gasped as her exploring hands neared the danger zone. "You just dislodged my toga. Honey, if you don't want to get into serious trouble," he whispered roughly, "maybe you'd better shift those hands of yours back north of the equator."

"What if I do want to get into serious trouble?"

She heard the sharp edge of his indrawn breath. Trembling, she felt his hands leave her breasts and trace a slow, lingering downward path until they encountered the edge of her short nightshirt. Slipping underneath, they circled around to cup her buttocks and pull her tightly against him.

There was no mistaking his intentions. The word was carnal. If he hadn't been holding her tightly, she wouldn't have been able to stand. Her knees were shaking. Her breath was coming so fast she was in danger of hyperventilating. "Please—" she gasped, knowing only that she wanted him more intensely than she had ever wanted anything in her entire life.

He began to edge away. Thinking he was leaving her, Mariah reached out to hold him and her hand accidentally brushed against his arousal. She gasped.

Gus groaned. Unable to help himself, he reached down and caught her fingers, closing them over the part of him that ached with hard need.

When she cried out, he swore softly and released her hand. "That was your right hand, wasn't it? Mariah, honey, I'm sorry."

She could have cried, and not from pain. "It's all right," she whispered, but the spell was broken. In another moment they would have been in bed together, swept along on a tide of passion more powerful than anything she had ever experienced.

Now it was gone. Come morning, Gus would be gone, too.

"I guess it's too much to hope we could go back to the beginning and start all over again?" Gus suggested, half hopefully, half teasing.

They both knew that was impossible. Being swept along on the floodtide of desire was one thing. Making the conscious decision to sleep together was something else. Not that he was a complete stranger to spontaneous combustion, but it had been a while. Back in his hell-raising college days, life had been a whole lot simpler.

Gus had far too much respect for Mariah to take what he wanted and then walk away. It wasn't that he was afraid she wouldn't enjoy it every bit as much as he did . . . well, almost as much, anyway. He was experienced enough to know that pleasing a woman only intensified his own pleasure.

But he had every intention of leaving. Come morning, he would be long gone. In a few more days he would be down on the Outer Banks, wrapped up in another building project, hassling red tape, material deliveries, the weather and probably the mosquitoes. By then he would have forgotten all about a woman and a baby down in some little nowhere town in east Georgia.

Yeah. Sure you will!

Seven

After a series of dreams that left him aching, empty and unsatisfied, Gus wakened to the smell of burning bacon, the sound of a crying baby. If he'd needed a sharp dose of reality, that served well enough.

By the time he appeared in the kitchen doorway, his shirt still not yet buttoned and his hair damp from two minutes under a shower that spat and dribbled luke-warm water, Mariah was bouncing a fussing Jessie on her left hip and turning bacon with a fork held awkwardly in two fingers and the thumb of her right hand.

"Oh, sorry if we woke you," she murmured.

"S'all right." Gus had his own morning routine. It had occasionally included a woman, but never a baby. "Can I help?"

"Want to feed Jessie? It's all fixed. I was trying to have something ready in case you were in a hurry to leave, but things got a bit confused." She smiled, and Gus thought it was damned unfair for any woman to look so enticing under the circumstances. Her bathrobe had seen better days. Her hair was in a shaggy braid down her back and her face was shiny, completely innocent of any hint of makeup.

She looked good enough to eat.

His stomach growled suddenly, and he scowled, as if scowling could deny his salacious thoughts. "Come on, possum, let Uncle Gus give you your breakfast."

"Possum?"

"She likes it. We understand each other, don't we, possum?" Jessie was no problem. Jessie he could handle. What had him worried was what had happened last night.

And, dammit, it was happening all over again!

The woman was a witch. He was hungry as a bear. He hadn't had his morning coffee, yet all it had taken was one look at the way her bathrobe slid over her hips when she moved and he started figuring out ways to get her out of it.

Only by turning his attention to the baby did he manage to rein in his baser appetites. "Okay, possum, let's try some of this yellow stuff. Open wide and give me a big target, will you? Attagirl!"

While Mariah scrambled eggs, Gus poked strained apricots into Jessie's hungry maw, grinning at the eager way she leaned into every spoonful. Between spoonfuls, she grinned right back at him.

"Amazing," he muttered.

"What's amazing?" Mariah brushed against his shoulder as she leaned over to place a bowl of what looked like wet plaster beside him. "This is some kind of baby cereal," she said. "She gets that next—or maybe it was supposed to be before. Basil explained, but I might have got the order wrong."

"Don't sweat it, it's all headed in the same direction." Scraping the jar, Gus prided himself that he was beginning to get the hang of this baby business. "We'll manage just fine, won't we, Jess?" Momentarily distracted by the mixed essence of fried bacon, lilac-scented soap and warm woman, Gus scraped the last spoonful from the jar and held it out. "You know, I've never been around many babies before, but I'm pretty sure Jessie's smarter than your average kid. Watch how she looks right into my eyes and smiles, like she's sharing a joke or something. There . . . y'see that? She likes me!"

Leaning her elbows on the table, Mariah used the bib to wipe a smear of apricots from Jessie's tiny chin. "Amazing," she teased. "And you think that makes her smart?"

Gus yanked her braid, and laughing softly, Mariah removed the empty apricot jar and shoved the bowl of cereal closer. She was using her hand a little more each day, but it was still sore and badly discolored.

While Mariah poured coffee, Gus loaded a spoon with the wet plaster, grinning when Jessie leaned forward eagerly. "Hey, slow down, small stuff. Uncle Gus can't shovel any faster." As Mariah moved back to the counter, he glanced after her and was struck by the way the shaft of sunshine slanting through the kitchen window highlighted her profile. Beauty might be only skin deep, but that didn't make it any less beautiful, which, he told himself, was a pretty profound thought for seven twenty-two in the morning.

Jessie didn't care for wet plaster. She pushed it out with her tongue, a look of such patent disgust on her small face that Gus could only marvel at the range of her emotions. "Ri?"

"Hmm?" Mariah was getting out the cream. It was canned.

"I don't think she likes this stuff."

"Oh? Then don't eat it, dumpling."

"Is that okay?" Gus was worried. "Maybe if you put more sugar in it?"

Mariah shot him a withering look. "Is that your answer to everything? More sugar?" Their eyes caught and held, and Gus was amazed to see a flush of warm color stain her cheeks. Was she thinking what he was? That some things were sweeter than any amount of sugar?

"Just trying to be helpful," he said with a shrug.

Still trying to be helpful, Gus found himself a few hours later sizing up the job of repairing her front step, having discovered a shed in the backyard filled with odds and ends of usable lumber. All it took was the thought of Mariah, with Jessie in her arms, stepping on that rotten plank and having it give way under their combined weight, to keep him from hitting the road right away.

He figured the job would take about an hour—two hours, tops. Then, too, there was the commode. He might as well fix that before he left. And the sink drain. And the door that wouldn't latch because the frame had sagged out of alignment.

He flat-out refused to think about all those stains on the ceiling. Damned if he was going to hang around long enough to reroof her house!

"Gus, I feel awful about this," Mariah protested, watching him carry an array of small tools from the locker in his truck bed, and then proceed to drag out scraps of building materials from the shed that had been on the verge of collapse for years.

Gus wondered if she had any idea what a distraction she was in a pair of baggy shorts and a man's shirt. If she didn't get out of his line of sight pretty soon, he couldn't guarantee his good behavior—especially when good behavior was the last thing on his mind.

She left, and he breathed a sigh of relief. He unfolded his six-foot ruler and measured the length of a cypress board.

"Here, I brought you some iced tea."

He dropped the rule, grappled for it on the ground, and slowly straightened, deliberately not letting his gaze stray to her long, bare legs. "Hmm...yeah. Thanks. Is it, um, sweetened?"

"Practically preserved. I know your tastes by now." Her smile shorted out a few more circuits in his brain, and for the life of him, he couldn't figure out why. Her teeth were good, but they weren't perfect. One of the two front ones lapped slightly over the other. Gus found the small flaw irresistible.

"Where's Jessie?" he asked gruffly.

"She fell asleep in her high chair. I mopped her off and put her down for a nap. Basil says she doesn't always take them, but to take advantage of it when it happens."

She dropped down onto the back stoop, and Gus slanted a quick look at the way she sat: back curved, head tilted to one side, arms wrapped around her long, graceful legs. With any other woman—with Lisa, for instance—it would be deliberate. Lisa was a great one for striking a pose. He'd told her about Lisa over supper last night after she'd confided a few details of her great romance with a tractor salesman who was looking for a live-in baby-sitter. Actually, he'd sort of made a joke of it.

"Believe it or not, I actually bought her a ring. Trouble was, while I was working up my nerve to pop the question, Lisa was busy arranging a modeling career in New York. Pretty funny, huh?"

"She's a model?" Mariah had asked. "Which agency?"

He'd shrugged. "If she ever said, I forgot. Models and I don't mix." She'd given him an odd look, then served the dessert.

That had been last night. Now, rising, he ambled over to the shed and beamed his flashlight into the cluttered interior. "Hey, you sure it's okay to use this stuff?"

"Nobody else ever will. Basil lives in an apartment, and none of my sisters is interested in building anything more than a career. And by the way, while you're dragging stuff out of the shed, if you see any garden tools, how about setting them outside. I'm missing a mattock."

"Yesterday when you said you liked gardening, I sort of pictured you wearing one of those big hats ladies wear and maybe a long, wispy dress, wandering through a bunch of flowers with a basket and a pair of shears in your hand."

When she threw back her head and laughed, Gus felt a powerful urge to laugh with her. "I didn't know you read fairy tales," she teased. "Which reminds me, while Jessie's asleep, this would be a good time to unpack my books."

Gus watched her go out of sight, then mopped the perspiration from his face with the back of his forearm. If he was smart—and the jury was still out on that one—he'd mend her steps, fix her plumbing and head for the hills before he got in any deeper. Before he wasted any more time thinking about things he'd sworn off thinking about.

On the other hand, he couldn't start hammering until Jessie woke up. Might as well check out the plumbing while he waited.

"Oh, good," Mariah said when he told her. "I've got a wrench in the lower right kitchen cabinet drawer, and as long as you're going to be inside anyway, could you listen out for Jessie for me? I need to run downtown for a few minutes."

Gus said sure, although the nearest thing to a downtown he'd seen was roughly forty-five miles away. Watching her back out the pinestraw-covered driveway, he thought about her bald tires and wondered if she could afford to replace them. Just how bad was she hurting for money, anyway? She'd said she was between jobs.

How many job opportunities could there be in a village that consisted, as far as he could tell, of a dozen or so frame houses, a general store, her hardware store, a garage, a couple of churches and a few ramshackle piers jutting out into a river he could spit across on a windless day?

While Mariah was gone, Gus shut off the water and traced the lines to a well pump that looked even older than the house. He usually subcontracted plumbing, but it didn't take an expert to tell him her pipes were shot, the foot valve in her pump was waterlogged, and she needed a new float valve in her commode tank.

He wondered if her famous Feed, Seed and Hardware Emporium boasted a plumbing department.

The lady's problems are none of your business, man. You're out of here, remember?

The trouble was, she puzzled him, and Gus had never been able to resist a puzzle. A woman with her kind of thoroughbred looks could easily make it as a model. Hell, if she could read a cue card, she might even wind up with her own TV show.

So what was she doing wasting her life in a nowhere place like Muddy Landing, looking after nieces and nephews and slaving away at some two-bit country store?

Late that afternoon Gus was still working on the front steps. Mariah had had mixed feelings when he'd declared that as long as he was at it, he might as well do the job right. There was lumber enough in the shed, left over from one of her father's old projects that had never got off the ground. Con Brady had been a great one when it came to starting things—including a family. Not so great when it came to following through.

She thought about that now, about how it had been having her father at home. The good and the bad. About how it had been later on, after he'd gone and her mother had disappeared into the bottle and never really surfaced again.

She thought about that stolen moment in the darkness with Gus, and told herself it had been a fluke, an accident. Because she hadn't been kissed in such a long time, and never like that, she'd simply overreacted.

A woman, after all, had certain needs.

She thought about Vance Brubaker and the dreams she had briefly harbored. Thank goodness she was wise enough now to realize that dreams were too fragile to survive the light of day.

No doubt a man like Gus had needs, too, she mused. He'd probably known so many women he would need a directory to sort them out. Not long ago, according to his own admission, he'd been on the verge of getting himself engaged. Whatever else his Lisa was, she was a fool.

"I'll cook you a good supper," she promised while she held one end of a board for him to saw. It was the least she could do. She certainly couldn't afford to pay him, not until she found another job.

They talked about that over fried chicken, grits, and collards from her garden, stir-fried with cracklings, and then smothered and steamed to bring out the sweetness.

"While I was in town this morning, I stopped by Grover's—the hardware store? I hadn't expected to get my own job back, but I thought maybe he might need a clerk. But he said the rumors are true. They're closing down now that that new hardware chain is building a place in Darien."

"So what'll you do?"

She shrugged. "I'll find something." She would have to. She simply couldn't go back to Vic. No matter how good the money was, she would never really be able to fit into that kind of fast, glitzy life.

Another few months and she wouldn't have been able to fit in anywhere. Not here in Muddy Landing, not after having lived in a place where the plumbing always worked. Where she could pick up a phone and order out when she was too tired to cook. Not after having a doorman open the door when she came home loaded with all her bags and parcels, and certainly not after receiving flowers and candy and exciting invitations from well-dressed men who drove big, fancy cars.

But she could never be happy living in New York or Palm Beach, either. Not when she was judged solely by her looks and by whose designs she wore, as if Sara Mariah Brady was solely the creation of Vic Chin, master manipulator. Not when the flattering invitations to dinner came with a price she was unwilling to pay.

"What were you doing down in Florida, anyway? You mentioned a job."

Gus's question startled her. It was as if he'd read her thoughts. If Gus liked her—and it was becoming more and more obvious to her that he did—she wanted it to be for who she was, not what she looked like. "I worked down there for almost a year. Actually, my work included some traveling, but I won't be going back. I don't particularly like to fly, and I'm not all that comfortable in big cities. I guess that sounds silly in this day and age, doesn't it?"

Gus reached across the table for the bowl and helped himself to the last of the collards. "Not especially. I don't like being herded onto a small range with a lot of strangers, either. Depends on what you're used to, I guess. I grew up in Durham, but now even Durham's about to outgrow me."

Again, Gus insisted on washing the dishes. Jessie was playing quietly in her playpen, fascinated by the set of keys Gus had given her after washing them off first, to Mariah's amusement.

"It's not as if she hasn't sampled everything in my house she could get her hands on, including the floor."

"Yeah, well, never let it be said that Gus Wydowski poisoned a lady with dirty keys." He grinned, and Mariah tried to store up the memory of how his eyes twinkled when he smiled, the way his teeth flashed white against his dark beard.

She reached past him to get what was left of the cake he'd bought, and Gus made the tactical mistake of reaching up and catching her around the wrist. Slowly, he stood and raked back his chair. By the sharp intake of her breath, he knew she was remembering the same thing he was.

Last night. The two of them together. Both catching fire, both so damned needy they could hardly stand up.

Abruptly he backed away. Raking a hand through his hair, he blew out his breath and said, "Sorry. I guess I don't want any cake after all."

"Gus, don't be embarrassed," Mariah said gently, but firmly enough so he would know she had her emotions under control. "We happen to... well, to affect each other that way. It's nothing that couldn't happen to anyone, given the right circumstances. It certainly doesn't mean anything."

"You know I wouldn't hurt you for the world, Mariah."

"I know that. Gus, you're a real nice man and a good friend. It would be a shame to let a little thing like...like physical attraction ruin our friendship. Who knows, you might just pass this way again and need a place to lay over. I wouldn't want you to be embarrassed to stop by."

"Yeah, well . . ." He stroked the back of his neck, kneading away the sudden tension that had gathered there. "It always pays to keep your options open, I guess," he said, while his eyes said something altogether different. Something that made Mariah's heart trip into double time.

But then, Jessie lost the keys through the slats of the playpen and asked for help in the only way she knew.

Gus reached for them at the same time that Mariah did. Their hands touched, and once again the sparks flew. She caught her breath sharply. "You said something about trying to get as far north as Savannah?"

"That was yesterday. What about Jessie? Are you up to lugging her around with one hand? What if you have to go somewhere? You don't even have a car seat yet." He'd meant to call, but never got around to it.

"I drove all the way home without a driver's license, remember? I think I can explain the lack of a car seat if I have to."

Gus tossed the keys into the pen and turned to her, an excess of emotion translating to anger. "Dammit, woman, we're not just talking about a ticket, we're talking about Jessie! Just because you're too pigheaded to admit you still need help—"

"If I need help, there are any number of people I can call on. I have friends in Muddy Landing, believe it or not."

Behind them, Jessie studiously fingered the dozen or so keys on the ring. Finding the one she was searching for, she gummed it contentedly while Gus and Mariah glared at each other.

Mariah gave in first. She sighed heavily. "All right, if you insist, I'll call Basil's answering service and leave word for him to have a car seat delivered. He's into computers. People with computers can send anything anywhere."

"They use car seats on the information highway?" Gus quirked a brow, wanting to take her in his arms. Not quite daring to touch her. She looked tired and worried and fragile, which only made him want her more. If there was one thing he'd always been a sucker for, it was a woman who needed him. *Anything* that needed him. Which meant he usually ended up getting in way over his head, he reminded himself.

"Look, why don't I stick around until tomorrow, and we'll see what can be had around these parts. Even people in Muddy Landing have babies and cars, don't they?"

It was hours later, long after Mariah had put Jessie down for the night and turned in herself, that Gus's restlessness drove him into the living room. TV was a washout. Freaks interviewing freaks. A science-fiction movie about creatures with heads that resembled English walnuts.

He switched it off and picked up yesterday's newspaper, then put it down again. The place was a mess, but oddly enough, it was a comfortable mess. Kind of homey. Gus couldn't remember the last time he'd thought in terms of "homey."

There was still that damned box of books, though. He'd manhandled it in and out of her car, in and out of her motel room—at least he could unpack the thing and get it out of her living room. No telling when she'd get around to unpacking it, what with the baby, and her hand still bothering her.

Raking aside a few old books and a collection of whatnots on the oak shelves, he made room and began taking out books, hardback and paperback, a handful at a time. He was about two layers down when he found the album. It never even occurred to him not to open it, and once he did, there was no turning back.

A couple squinting in the sun, standing beside a 1950 Pontiac. Her parents? The man was tall, the woman small. She stood in his shadow, literally and probably figuratively. There were several more snapshots of the woman with two kids, a boy and a girl. No more of the man. One of the woman with the two kids and a baby on her lap. Gus figured the baby must be Burdina, the boy obviously Basil. He'd looked like a nerd even then. The tallest kid had to be Mariah. For a long time he studied the skinny little girl in the sagging dress, with the tight braids and the knobby knees. She wore glasses. She hadn't been a pretty child, he could tell that much even though she was looking down at her bare feet in most of the pictures.

Poor kid, her mama hadn't even bothered to tie a bow on the ends of her pigtails. Probably hadn't had time.

Gus leafed through the album, lingering over all the pictures he could find of Mariah. There weren't many. After a few more pages the woman disappeared and most of the pictures were of the school variety. None of the kids, so far as Gus could see, bore any resemblance to the Mariah he knew. One of them—he figured it might be the one called Alethia—had the same delicately stubborn jaw that made Mariah's face so distinctive. The pair of them, he thought, must have been a handful.

He was closing the book when the two eight-by-ten glossies slipped out. They were professional shots, obviously not a part of the family album. He started to shove them back in place when a familiar pair of legs caught his attention. Long, lean, glistening with oil, they were made even longer by one of those bathing suits that was cut all the way up to the waist.

The model was standing on a beach, the wind blowing her hair across her face, blowing an oversize, transparent top that was held together by a single finger against her body. The top part of her face was covered by her hair, leaving only a portion of it visible. A portion that included a wide, sweetly curved mouth and a firm but delicate jaw.

Gus swore softly. Anger shot through him, bitter as gall. With bleak eyes, he stared down at the two photos, the other one not quite so revealing, and then he slid them back inside the album and placed it back in the box.

Eight

———

They got it all out in the open the following morning. Gus felt like the very devil. He hadn't slept until nearly daylight, and then he'd thought about Dina, who had broken his heart nearly twenty years ago, and Lisa, who had bruised his ego only a few weeks ago. He dreamed the pair of them had pulled up to the bank of the Little Charlie River in a yacht the size of an aircraft carrier and asked for Gus.

He'd tried to tell them he was Gus, but they'd laughed and told him to go find Gus, and then he'd found himself on a scaffold trying to find his way into the second story of a two-story house that had neither stairs nor windows.

All in all, he'd had better dreams.

"Were you going to tell me about your other career, or are you into playing games?" He'd confronted Mariah the moment she'd entered the kitchen, angry because she'd deceived him, angry because he didn't want to care. And he did.

"My other— Oh. You mean modeling. How did you find out?"

Gus's sneer would have done credit to a B-movie villain. "You mean, I wasn't supposed to find those pictures? I thought that was why you'd left the box sitting out so long."

"Oh, Gus, for heaven's sake. I left it out because with everything stacked out of Jessie's reach, I didn't have room to unpack it. And anyway, what difference does it make?"

"That's what you were doing down in Florida, right?"

"So?" Her tone dared him to make something of it.

"So? So what's the big secret? What was all that garbage about being a clerk in a hardware store?"

"I worked at Grover's store for twelve years—more than that, if you count a part-time job after school. I was a model for less than a year."

"Why'd you quit?"

She looked at him as if he'd lost his wits. "Because Basil needed me. You know that."

"There has to be another reason. No woman walks away from a modeling career just to baby-sit her brother's kid."

"Well, this one did."

"But you're going back, right? All this business about looking for a job around here . . . it's so much moonshine, isn't it?"

"Do you want bacon or sausage with your eggs?"

"Sausage! Are you going back, or aren't you?"

"Whether I do or not, it's nothing to do with you. I'm not Lisa."

No, she wasn't Lisa. Mariah was . . . well, she was Mariah. Which was one of the reasons this thing had hit him so hard.

And then she dropped the iron skillet. It slipped out of her right hand, landed on the floor, and cartwheeled over onto Gus's foot. He swore, snatched up the heavy pan and set it on the stove. "Go sit down, I'll make breakfast," he growled. "I told you you were trying to do too much with that hand of yours! You can't even take care of yourself, much less a kid!"

Furious, Mariah stalked out.

Frustrated, Gus watched her go.

The next two days were both strange and strained. Gus found one excuse after another to hang around. Tempers sparked and then fizzled. They quarreled over nothing at all, apologized and then quarreled again. Gus told himself it was like being married with all the responsibilities and none of the perks, and increasingly, it was the perks he wanted.

Sharing the small intimacies of daily living with Mariah left him in a near constant state of arousal, which was how he rationalized his short temper.

He wondered what *her* excuse was.

Forcing himself to ignore his most pressing masculine instincts, Gus repaired ancient plumbing, replaced a section of railing on the small back stoop, and soldered several pinhole leaks in the old copper pipes. He thought of a dozen reasons to leave and two dozen reasons to stay.

As her hand slowly mended, Mariah dug up shrubs from one side of the yard and replanted them on the other. Gus thought she was slightly nuts. Even so, it was all he could do to keep from removing the spade from her hands, laying her down on the sweet-smelling pinestraw, and making love to her until neither of them could remember all the reasons why they shouldn't.

Basil checked in a couple of times. He'd found Myrtiss. They were working things out. Jessie was a constant source of amazement. Gus knew next to nothing about babies, but he was learning fast. Twice he drove into town to the hardware store and the cluttered country store that passed for a supermarket in a village of several hundred souls. There he had ample opportunity to observe other members of the human species in the larval stage.

"Y'know, I notice some babies are pretty noisy. Screaming, whining, kicking up a fuss at the least little thing. Is that normal?" he asked. They'd both been working outside; Mariah hanging laundry on the clothesline he'd mended and then pulling up handfuls of chickweed, Gus shoring up the shed that was threatening to tumble in on itself. Now they were taking a break.

"I'm no expert," she murmured lazily, her eyes closed against the sun. "I suppose babies are just like anyone else. Some whine. Some don't."

Gus leaned back, placing his elbows on the step above the one on which he sat, which, incidentally, gave him an excellent view of the top of Mariah's head and her long, muddy-kneed legs on the steps below. "Jessie doesn't whine, do you, possum blossom? When Miss Jessie wants something, she maps out a plan of action and then puts it in gear. This morning, while you were in the shower, I watched her set her sights on that wastebasket over by the green-striped chair. She thought about it for a few minutes—you could practically see the wheels turning—then, damned if she didn't slide down off the sofa, grab the coffee table and work her way around so she could grab hold of the chair, and then she—"

"Gus, you didn't let her reach it, did you? Darn it, you know she eats everything she gets her hands on!"

He was in no mood to fight. "Tell me about it," he said dryly, combing his beard with his fingers. The little dickens had yanked on it, chewed on it and massaged a good part of every meal into it. She got more food on his outside than she did her own inside. He'd been down to his last clean shirt this morning.

Eyeing the line of freshly washed clothes flapping in the soft Georgia breeze, he knew a moment of embarrassment. While he was in the shower, Mariah had gathered up his clothes and tossed them into the washer along with her own and Jessie's. Now, there they hung, together in all their intimacy—her skimpies, his boxers, her sweats, his khakis, a row of Jessie's tiny garments and three of his shirts.

Sunlight shafted down from the pines and the tall, moss-hung cypress trees that shaded a good portion of her backyard. "Your pines are dripping all over my truck," he said, lacking the energy to move both vehicles around back.

"Sorry. Sap's rising."

Boy, was it ever! In an effort to quell his own rising sap, Gus inhaled the mingled scent of resin, damp earth and the rich, marshy essence of the nearby river. From somewhere in the distance came the rapid-fire sound of a woodpecker. Actually, Muddy Landing wasn't half bad, he decided. Quiet, peaceful. The kind of place that lagged half a century behind the rest of the world. A guy could get addicted to this kind of life. . . .

Which was just one more sign that he'd better start thinking about moving on before he got sucked in any deeper. No woman who had tasted the kind of life she obviously had would be content with life in a small town for very long.

He glanced at the playpen where Jessie, a plastic mixing bowl forgotten on her head, studiously examined a muddy, starfish-shaped hand. She'd been reaching out through the playpen fence, sampling the dirt on all four sides. Gus figured it was probably pretty clean dirt after all the rain they'd had.

Once the rain had stopped, the weather had turned unseasonably warm. Made a man lazy—too lazy to fight. Too lazy even to fight off temptation, when he knew damn well there was no future in it.

His gaze shifted to where Mariah lay sprawled in drowsy abandon on the steps below him. She was wearing a pair of baggy shorts and a man's shirt, one bare foot toying with the handle of her spade. He pictured her the way she'd looked in that eight-by-ten glossie, her legs exposed up to her waist and that sexy, see-through top held with one finger.

This was even sexier. She'd piled her hair up on top of her head and now it was sliding down in curling tendrils. Her skin—or at least, the parts of it that were visible—had already turned a deeper shade of ivory from working outdoors in the dappled sunlight. Gus thought he'd never in all his born days seen anything quite so delectable as the shallow valley of her nape.

"I'd better do something about lunch," she murmured, stirring reluctantly. "I'm beginning to feel a mite peckish."

"Yeah, and I'd better finish up the shed and think about heading north."

He was beginning to feel a mite peckish, too, but he had an idea they were talking about two different kinds of hunger. Every morning since he'd arrived, he had made up his mind to leave before the day ended. Last night he'd almost split without even saying goodbye.

Yet here he was. He tried to tell himself it was because of Jessie—because a scrap of blue-eyed mischief in baggy diapers had dug herself a place in his heart and refused to get out—but he knew better. He'd fallen under the spell of a woman who made it too easy to believe what he wanted to believe and not what experience had taught him.

Once bitten, they said, twice shy. Gus had been bitten once too often. This time he knew better than to get within striking distance.

At supper that night Jessie was fretful, which wasn't at all like her. After flinging handfuls of liver and green beans in all directions, she deliberately threw her bowl to the floor, then glared at Gus, her stubborn little chin set in a way that reminded him of her Aunt Ri. Her big blue eyes seemed to say, "Go ahead, sucker, make my day."

Gus was on to her methods. Women were women, even in the infant stage. "Listen, possum, if I didn't think you'd enjoy it too much I'd make you climb down out of that contraption and clean up the mess yourself." His gruff tone was nullified by the big, gentle hand that was tenderly holding one small, fat foot.

"Let me," Mariah said tiredly, rising just as Gus did. After washing and hanging clothes, she'd spent the rest of the day moving plants. To Gus's untutored eyes, the yard didn't look any better than it had when she'd started out, but then, he was no more expert on landscaping than he was on babies. Maybe he would get Angel to send her some books.

They both reached for Jessie at the same time, and their arms tangled. Automatically, he steadied her by clasping her upper arms, and for one brief moment she allowed her head to fall tiredly forward onto his shoulder.

Gus shut his eyes and struggled with his private demons. "You're asleep on your feet," he accused softly.

"Too much digging. I'm out of practice. Yoga just doesn't do it for me anymore, not that it ever did."

Yoga? He hadn't a clue what she was talking about. At the moment, he didn't care. It was all he could do to resist the urge to sweep her into his arms and carry her off to the nearest bed. He'd seen electromagnets less powerful than this thing, whatever it was, that had sprung up between them.

Mariah sighed. "I'd better get her bathed and into bed. If she's coming down with something, I'm going to have to track Basil down and find out what to do. Maybe she's just cutting another tooth. Do you think that could be it?"

"I expect that's all that's wrong with her," Gus said, trying to sound as if he knew what he was talking about. He'd noticed she was favoring her right hand again. He'd warned her not to go at it so hard, but once the woman got a shovel in her hands, she was unstoppable. "Look, you just peel her down and run her a bath while I put the dishes in to soak. I'll take it from here. You got anything to drink? You look like you could use a good muscle relaxant."

"Gus, you don't have to—"

"Don't waste energy arguing. Now, march! *Hup*-two, *hup*-two!"

He watched her collect a grizzling Jessie and tried not to be affected by the way her shoulders sagged, by the shadows under her eyes. He had an idea she might have gotten up a few times during the night. Sleeping in the same room with a fussy baby, it would be hard not to.

He wished now he'd never confronted her with those damned pictures and demanded to know what kind of a game she was playing.

Wished he'd never even found the things.

Furthermore, that jerk, Basil, had no right to dump his kid off on a woman who'd just been through a mugging, had her hand busted, been forced to spend a night in a motel with a stranger, and then had to drive herself all the way home. Gus would never dream of imposing on his own sister the way this Basil guy did Mariah. Sure, Angel might do a little mending for him whenever he stopped off in Durham for a visit. She even cooked him the occasional meal, but he always took care to return the favor. Hell, he'd practically rebuilt her whole house!

What had this Basil guy ever done for Mariah, besides leave her here to wither away in the wilderness, at the mercy of any smooth-talking tractor salesman who happened by? Was that any way to treat a lady?

Hell, no, it wasn't! Stacking dishes haphazardly in the sink, Gus ran scalding water over them and made up his mind that tomorrow he was going to locate a locksmith and have every lock in her house changed. Next he would find an appliance store and buy her a dishwashing machine. And a dryer, while he was at it. A woman like Mariah, whether or not she ever returned to modeling, had no business holed up here in the swamp, with the nearest neighbor a bee-keeping old hermit who lived almost a mile down the road.

She was ruining her hands washing clothes and dishes, letting her face get all chapped and sunburned from grubbing in the yard and hanging her wash out on a line.

It never occurred to him that Mariah might not appreciate his gifts. Gus had always been generous with his women, buying them gifts of jewelry, perfume, candy, flowers...even clothing. Lisa had had a weakness for expensive lingerie, big blue opals and good champagne.

So maybe the things Mariah needed right now happened to be a little more practical than they were romantic. What difference did that make?

Leaving the dishes to soak, he took over Jessie's bath, edging Mariah aside to kneel beside the bathtub. "Don't try to lift her with that hand of yours, she's slippery as an eel. Here, let Uncle Gus take care of—hey, don't eat the soap, possum! It doesn't taste half as good as it smells."

"Eel? Possum? She's going to have an identity crisis if you're not careful." Mariah held a towel and Gus lifted the baby onto her lap. "Hand me the powder, will you?"

Frowning, he watched her stand the baby on her lap and slap baby powder on her tiny pink rear end. Worried, he watched as she fastened on a diaper and tugged a minuscule undershirt over her head. As a rule, Jessie enjoyed the whole process, but tonight nothing seemed to suit her. She seemed to want to chew on everything.

"I think I was right about the tooth," Mariah murmured, and he nodded sagely. "Her gum looks a little swollen, right there, see?"

Together, they settled her with a bottle, and then Gus finished the dishes. Deliberately, he forced himself to think about the job waiting for him on the coast. Two cottages, each in the two-hundred-and-fifty-thousand-dollar range, was a plum for any contractor. ATW Construction had an excellent record for finishing up under budget and ahead of schedule. After years of struggling to get established, he could more or less choose his clients now, varying jobs between the coast and the mountains. There was nothing to tie him down to any one location. He had a good working relationship with building inspectors, subcontractors, suppliers and county bureaucrats in both ends of the state. He was a free-ranging bachelor with no dependents, and he liked his life just fine the way it was.

And if he knew what was good for him, he thought ruefully, he'd get back to business and forget a certain woman who was not only a major puzzle, but a major distraction.

It was impossible to sleep. Gus thought maybe he'd caught his restlessness from Jessie. He lay awake on an unfamiliar bed in an unfamiliar bedroom, on sheets that smelled of sunshine instead of laundry detergent. With the window open, he could hear the faint whisper of wind in the pines, and the soft, curious cry of a barn owl.

At home he would be listening to the sound of the small spring that tumbled over a rocky ledge just outside his window. At the coast, he would be hearing the soothing sound of the surf.

Oboy. A place like this could screw up a man's thinking before he even knew what had hit him. What was that old song about "Georgia On My Mind"?

Time to move on, he thought for the hundredth time. He'd get a good night's sleep, make a few calls in the morning, and then head north. Thus having settled things in his mind, Gus set about forcing his body to relax.

Gus never knew how much later it was when he came wide awake, hearing the plaintive sound of Jessie's whimper, the soft sound of Mariah's murmured response. He was out of bed like a shot. This time he took the time to step into a pair of khakis and zip them up.

"What's wrong?" he whispered, hurrying into the room next door. "Is she sick?"

"Shh, no, she doesn't feel feverish. I'm pretty sure she's just cutting another tooth. Basil said it made her cranky. She's been chewing on everything even more than usual."

Mariah sat on the edge of the bed, holding the baby in her arms. Humming tunelessly under her breath, she swayed back and forth.

Gus tiptoed into the living room and returned a moment later with a rocking chair that looked about ready for a three-thousand-mile checkup. "Here, this'll be easier on your back," he said. He lifted the baby and waited until Mariah was seated in the rocker, placed her in her arms and then sat on the edge of the bed.

"You don't have to stay. Go back to bed," Mariah whispered.

"You might need something."

Mariah did need something, but she didn't think Gus was ready to supply it. For all the help he had been, he'd be leaving most any day now. He'd been threatening to leave ever since he'd pulled into her driveway.

The past week had been a learning experience. Unfortunately, she hadn't learned until it was too late that playing house with a man and a baby could be hazardous to a woman's health.

Especially when that man was Gus Wydowski.

It was almost funny, she mused sadly as she rocked and hummed, while Gus watched from the edge of her rumpled bed. In the faint glow of a pink night-light he looked tough and untamed, completely out of his element. Which, oddly enough, made him seem almost vulnerable. He would never in this world have made it as a male model, and yet . . .

As a girl, Mariah had dreamed the usual dreams about growing up and being swept off her feet by a handsome prince and living happily ever after. Pity she hadn't realized until it was too late that not all princes were handsome and wealthy and well-dressed and charming. Some were shaggy and bearded and tough, with callused hands and baggy khakis and smiles so sweet they melted their way right into a woman's heart before she could defend herself.

"She's asleep," Gus whispered, and she nodded sadly, not quite ready to relinquish the satisfaction of holding a baby's warm body close to her heart. If that was all she could hold...

"I'll put her down," he said, and she stood, sensing something in the quiet purposefulness of his voice that set her pulse to pounding so hard she could actually hear the sound.

Mariah had had Basil put the crib in her own room to make sure she would hear if Jessie wakened in the night. Now she folded back the rabbit-print spread, and stood back for Gus to put her down.

The pale light gleamed on his broad back as he leaned over the crib, and Mariah marveled all over again at what a strange man he was. To think she'd once suspected he might be an escaped or newly released prisoner. He'd lost his pallor now that he'd finally found a few days of sun. She fancied he'd even gained a pound or two, thanks to her good country cooking.

He touched her arm, sensitizing every nerve ending in her body. "Come on, let's get out of here so she can settle down again."

"Go to bed, Gus." Had that thin, wavering voice come from her throat?

"Mariah."

She shivered. If she followed him out of the room, she was afraid of what might happen. Afraid it would—even more afraid it wouldn't. Ever since he'd kissed her outside that miserable little convenience store in Florida, something had been building between them. Maybe it was time to turn and face the music.

Gus turned and walked out. After only the briefest hesitation, Mariah took a deep breath, followed him into the hall and closed the door quietly behind her.

He was standing just outside the door. Wordlessly, he opened his arms and, as the last shred of common sense she possessed faded like river mist under a hot summer sun, Mariah moved into his embrace.

No more waiting, she thought with a feeling made of equal parts apprehension and relief. He was going to kiss her again, and she was going to kiss him right back. They were going to make love, and she suspected she might wake up alone a few hours from now. By next week—by next month—she might even be able to convince herself she had dreamed the whole thing.

So be it.

"Tonight," Gus whispered as his arms closed around her. "Just give me tonight and I won't ask for more."

Ask! Ask! she cried silently.

Gus never knew which one of them made the first move, but suddenly his mouth found hers and he was backing her into the room he slept in. He was shaking so hard he could scarcely walk. *Get a grip, Wydowski! Don't blow it now!*

He bumped against a chair in the darkness, jostling them apart, and they both laughed a little breathlessly. He aimed a kiss for her mouth, missed and caught the side of her nose, so then he moved on to her eyes and her temple, and that was wonderful, too. Her hair smelled like sunshine and shampoo. Her skin was soft and smooth as butter and smelled of the lilac soap she used. He wanted to kiss her everywhere all at once, wanted to love every exquisite inch of her body — wanted to leave with a memory that would last them both long after this night.

Because after tonight, he would be gone. After tonight, he would have to go, else he might never be able to walk away. There was no future for them. Gus had been down this same road before, and he knew where it ended.

"Mariah," he whispered hoarsely, his lips buried in her throat as he urged her toward the bed.

"Shh, don't talk. I don't want to think about anything but this. Gus, just make love to me . . . please?"

Even knowing what he knew about her, he was surprised. Suddenly struck by a crazy notion, he said, "Mariah . . . you, uh, you have done this before, haven't you? I mean, you're not a—"

"A virgin?" She gave a husky little gasp of laughter. "Good gracious, of course not! I've had lots and lots of experience!" If one weekend in Savannah with a garden-tractor salesman who wore his socks to bed could be considered lots of experience. Before she'd even got airborne, Vance had been snoring. She'd never even got off the launch pad. "But, Gus, I'm not taking any pills or anything."

He laughed raggedly. "I'm not, either, but I've got something in my bag. Give me a minute, will you?" He needed the minute to pull himself together. Damn! He felt like a ton of black powder on a short fuse!

She was still standing beside the bed when he reached out again, still wearing her cotton nightgown. He'd never slept with a woman who wore cotton to bed. Most of them wore a few scraps of something sinfully sexy if they wore anything at all.

Slowly he lifted her gown up over her hips, over her breasts, over her head, savoring every whisper of cloth against skin. His khakis followed her gown to the floor. They were standing beside the bed, and he lowered her carefully and then came down beside her. He was shaking like a leaf. He'd wanted this since almost the first time he'd laid eyes on her. The feeling had intensified until it was all he could think about.

Now that fantasy was about to become reality, he didn't want to entertain any second thoughts.

As her eyes adjusted to the wisp of moonlight that flowed in through the open window like a silent silver tide, Mariah gazed up at his wide, powerful shoulders, at the dark, diamond-shaped thicket that covered his chest. Most of the men she'd known as a model shaved their bodies. She had never before realized just how exciting masculine body hair could be.

With a boldness that came from somewhere outside her experience, she reached up and touched his chest. Her fingernail scraped one of his flat nipples and it peaked instantly. She heard the sound of his sharply indrawn breath, felt him thrust against her lower body—knew a swift surge of pleasure that her touch could cause such a powerful reaction.

She longed to explore his body all over, but didn't quite dare. It took more than a few months' exposure to the glamorous, sophisticated world of modeling to overcome a lifetime of doubt and inhibition.

"Gus, I—"

"What, sweetheart? What do you like?"

"You," she said simply, and thrilled when he surged again. Her belly was pressed against him, their legs entwined. From the waist up, they leaned outward. Gus's gaze moved down over her breasts, and she inhaled deeply, wishing chest size could make up for a lack of breast size. Not that either measurement was much to brag about.

Gus thought she was the most exquisite woman he had ever known. The pictures had lied. The real Mariah was far more than a body put on display for the world to admire. More beautiful, more real and far more complex.

And tonight, for just a few hours, all this loveliness, all this sexiness, all this sweetness was his alone. After tonight—

But he wasn't going to think about after tonight.

She was so damned delicately made. "I don't want to hurt you, sweetheart." He trailed a fingertip over the swell of her breast, feeling the tight little bud pull even tighter under his caress. He heard her breath catch in her throat, felt a film of perspiration break out over his body.

"You won't hurt me, Gus. I'm not exactly fragile." She assayed a little laugh that didn't quite come off.

Fragile. She was that, all right, no matter what else she was. Brittle could be hard, but it could also be breakable. Gus desperately wanted to take it slow, to make it last, for both their sakes, but he wasn't sure just how long he could hang on. He could feel the heat of her against his groin, burning him, drawing him deeper and deeper under her spell.

"Wait, sweetheart," he rasped. "Wait a minute!" He eased back slightly, afraid of disgracing himself.

And then she reached her hand down between them. Her fingers curled around his shaft and she whispered, "Please, I want to touch you."

He nearly exploded. He must have made some sort of strangled sound, because she jerked her hand away as if she'd been burned.

She probably had. He was hot enough.

"Gus, please don't change your mind now," she whispered.

A mind? What was a mind? His aching, throbbing groin had a mind of its own. He took her mouth hungrily in a kiss that was feverish and hungry and achingly sensual. Fumbling in the darkness with one hand, he tried to rip open a small foil packet. It wasn't easy. Her legs were all around him, and she was hot and silky. The intoxicating essence of sex and lilacs drifted up around him, nearly driving him over the edge.

"Slow down, sweetheart," he grated. He wanted to touch her first, to bring her to readiness. He wanted to kiss her, to taste her, to fill his senses with the woman who was Sara Mariah Brady. To fill her senses with him.

But Mariah had no intention of slowing down. She knew in her heart that he would leave her tomorrow. Once, a wild bird had flown into a windowpane and fallen stunned to the ground. She'd been able to hold him for just a little while. But holding him for a fleeting moment hadn't made him tame. Nor had it made him hers.

Gus's hands moved down her body and she lifted her hips. Any small store of pride she had once possessed was long gone. She wanted him *now*. Needed him *now!* "Gus...please?"

And then he touched her in a way that made her explode into flames. Shuddering, she gasped his name just as he came inside her, and once again the earth began to spin out of control. Her eyes wide open, she stared up at him. In the dim, silvery light she saw the harsh set of his features, the look of pain that twisted his face into an unfamiliar mask. His breathing was raw, each separate breath broken by a series of small, shuddering gasps. He muttered something—prayer or profanity, she couldn't be sure. Then he collapsed on top of her.

She bore his weight willingly, wrapping him in her arms until he rolled over, pulling her with him, holding her the way a drowning man would hold on to a life raft.

To her amazement Mariah found that this was even sweeter in its own way than the wild explosion of pleasure that was so fierce it was almost unbearable.

"Yes-ss...." he whispered harshly.

Yes, she thought, knowing even then that the ultimate answer would be no.

Nine

Gus woke instantly. He'd been miles under for the first time in weeks—maybe in years. Good sex could do that for a man. Good, as in terrific. As in the best.

It was still pitch-dark outside. It's always darkest before the dawn. The words popped into his head, and he wondered who had said them. And then he wondered why it mattered.

What mattered was why he'd come clean out of a deep sleep when he knew damned well he hadn't set any alarm clocks.

Beside him, Mariah's breathing was slow and soft and regular. One of her arms was flung over his belly, her face buried against his shoulder. She smelled faintly of scented soap, faintly of sex. He felt himself growing hard all over again and wondered if he was up to another round. Wondered if she was too tender.

He hadn't gone easy on her, and he was pretty sure she wasn't nearly as experienced as she wanted him to believe.

But then, she hadn't gone easy on him, either. Especially not that last time.

He closed his eyes and let the memory of the past few hours flood over him again. The heat. The driving, striving, throbbing, aching urgency. And then the fiery, incredibly sweet release.

Sweet salvation. And he'd thought he knew it all. Thought there could be no more surprises.

It occurred to him that he couldn't remember the last time he had wakened with a woman in his bed that he didn't have a niggling sense of depression. No matter how good the sex had been. No matter that it had been between consenting adults who fully understood and appreciated basic biology. Not to mention basic reality.

Mariah stirred in her sleep and he looked down at her with a feeling uncomfortably close to possessiveness.

He felt good. Better than good, he felt *righteous!*

And then, "What the hell is that?" he muttered suddenly, freezing with his hand hovering over her breast.

That wasn't Jessie he'd heard. Not unless she was taking her crib apart slat by slat and throwing the pieces on the floor. Without even pausing to think, Gus slid silently out of bed. His foot tangled in his discarded khakis and he pulled them on and hastily zipped them up.

Good thinking, Wydowski. You don't want to walk into any surprise party with your bare facts hanging out.

"Stay put, sweetheart," he mouthed in the darkness when he heard Mariah murmur his name in her sleep. Moving swiftly, silently, he glanced in both directions along the hallway before easing into the room Jessie shared with Mariah.

The room smelled familiarly of woman things and baby things. In the dim glow from the pink night-light, he gazed down into the crib, feeling a powerful surge of protectiveness at the sight of Jessie's small body. She was sleeping soundly in her favorite position: belly down, butt in the air, one fist shoved into her mouth.

Gus pulled the rabbit-print spread up over her back, lingered another moment, then eased back out into the hall.

The sound of a muffled curse had him instantly flattening his body against the wall. He wasn't a gun-toting man, but at a time like this he wouldn't have minded the reassuring feel of a chunk of cold steel in his hands. He had a woman and a child to protect. And while he was pretty good with his fists, if there happened to be more than a couple of them, and if they happened to be armed, he just might find himself slightly overmatched.

There were at least two of them. They were in the living room. The lights were still off, but one of them had a penlight. From the noise they were making, he figured one of them was going through the drawers on the small chest that served as an end table. The other was over near the bookcase.

"Watch that footstool, Eddie. I nearly broke my neck fallin' over it," one of them said.

"Cripes, there ain't nothing in here but junk," another one muttered.

Junk, Gus thought wryly, that was piled, stacked and heaped out of reach of an extremely mobile eight-month-old baby. Jessie's taste for bric-a-brac was notorious.

"There's the woman. She weren't half bad, y'know."

"Too skinny. Me, I like more meat on my women."

Gus felt a sick lurch in his belly and a film of cold sweat on his brow. He would kill them with his bare hands.

"Hell, there ain't nothin' in here worth takin'! If you ain't up to no action, go out to the car. Me, I ain't leaving without a taste o' them skin an' bones. I'll warm 'er up, and if there's anything left when I git finished, you kin have it. But, man, we come all this way, an' I ain't walkin' outta here without somethin'!"

Over my dead body!

Gus swore. The sound carried.

"What was that?"

"Turn on a damn light, Buck!"

"What, an' have ever' neighbor in the woods comin' down on us?"

"There ain't no neighbors, dammit! This place is stuck so far out in the woods, don't nobody but muskrats even know where it's at! Now come on, the

bitch was carryin' near 'bout five hunnert bucks! You
wuz the one said there'd be plenny more where that
come from, so le's find it an' get the hell outta here!'"

Gus eased back into the kitchen. There on the shelf
by the back door was Mariah's toolbox. He had teased
her about the contents, but he wasn't laughing now.
The short section of conduit she used as a lever for
loosening outside valves just might, in the dark, pass
for the barrel of a gun.

If he'd known he was going to be facing down a
couple of scumbags, he would have armed himself
with something a lot more lethal than a length of gal-
vanized pipe. Like maybe his power nailer. A few
rounds from that should do the trick.

They were arguing so fiercely Gus was able to move
into position without being heard. With the wall at his
back, he said quietly, "Now, then...you guys want to
put your hands on your head and turn around real
slow? I'd sure appreciate your cooperation."

The reaction was ludicrous, to put it mildly. One of
them dropped whatever he'd had in his hands—Gus
thought it might've been the ceramic dogwood box
Mariah had transferred from the coffee table to the
top bookshelf, well out of Jessie's reach—at least until she figured out how to climb. On its way down, it
struck the handle of a small plastic lawnmower with
bells on the wheels, then hit the floor and broke with
a loud crash.

Calmly, Gus cut through a stream of gutter profanity. "I don't want to have to shoot you guys, because
you're out of season, and I don't have a license. On

the other hand, I guess it's always open season on vermin."

He congratulated himself on sounding laid-back. He wasn't. His blood pressure was fit to blow a gasket. His mouth tasted like gunmetal. All he could think of was that Jessie and Mariah were sleeping just a few feet down the hall.

Wrong.

"What is it, Gus?" Mariah whispered, startling him so that he nearly dropped his weapon.

"Nothing I can't handle, Ri, go back to bed."

"I thought I heard Jessie. Wait a minute, I'll turn on a light so—"

He caught her hand and squeezed hard. He thought it was her left hand. He hoped so. "No problem, honey, go on back to bed. If Jessie wakes up, *he's* going to want to get involved, and you know Jessie. The guy never did have much self-control."

He could almost hear the wheels spinning in her head.

Jessie—a guy?

"Back up, honey." *Backup! Make 'em think we've got backup!* "That is, go back into the kitchen and call the sheriff, will you? Looks like we caught us a couple of rats in our trap."

She was a quick study, he'd hand her that. In less than two minutes she had the law on the way. "Here, you hold the gun while I tie these jerks up. Careful now, the safety's off. Don't even breathe on that trigger."

Gus handed her the short length of pipe. Leaning close to her ear, he whispered, "Play along."

Then he moved swiftly to the kitchen, located a coil of leftover clothesline and grabbed a butcher knife out of the drawer. On his way back, he heard certain indications that Jessie wanted in on the act.

Oboy.

Some forty-five minutes later Gus heard the sheriff's car stop at the end of the dirt road, then take a left into town. The guy had been a little too curious about who he was and what he was doing there with Mariah in the middle of the night, but he'd kept his mouth shut.

Gus just hoped he would go on keeping it shut. Small towns were bad about gossip, even in this day and age, when the only rule was, there weren't any rules.

Slowly he began the process of coming down off an adrenaline high. His stomach growled, and he recognized the beginnings of a headache. He told himself that the good news was that the creeps who had snatched Mariah's purse and would've snatched a hell of a lot more, were in custody. And that she had her house keys back, even if her money was long gone.

The bad news was, it was raining again.

"We might as well have breakfast." Mariah leaned against the doorframe. She was wearing a yellow-flowered cotton bathrobe that had seen better days. On her, it looked like a million bucks. She had brushed her hair into a semblance of order, but she still didn't look ready to face another day.

Gus wondered if he was responsible for those shadows under her eyes. All things considered, they hadn't had a whole lot of rest.

"Jessie's too wide awake to go back to sleep now," she said. "I changed her and gave her a bottle, but it's not going to buy much more time, I'm afraid. If you're hungry, you'd better get on with breakfast."

He figured they'd been up for a couple of hours. It seemed like a lot longer than that. So far they'd avoided so much as a meeting of the eyes, much less any mention of what had happened between them a few hours ago.

Much less what it all meant.

Tension hung so heavy in the air Gus could almost taste it. That stubborn jaw of hers was all squared up for trouble. He watched her come to attention—chin up, back straight—just as if he hadn't intimately explored every vertebra in that long, elegant spine of hers.

As if she regretted what they'd done last night.

As if she wanted him out of there.

Gus fully intended to leave, but first he had a few things to say. He'd never been the type to sleep and run, and he wasn't about to start now. Besides which, being kicked out of any woman's life wasn't exactly his favorite way to start a day.

"Cereal will do for me," he said gruffly, avoiding her eyes by the simple expedient of rummaging in the silverware drawer.

"Fine. Then while you're eating, I'll shower and get Jessie up."

"Fine."

Dammit, she didn't have to act like they were still strangers! What had happened last night might not have signaled orange blossoms, in-laws—the whole damn long-term bit—but it had meant *something*.

At least, it had to him.

Gus put the coffee on to brew. He poured Honey-Nut Crunch in a bowl, sliced a banana on top, ladled a couple of spoonfuls of sugar on top of that, and wet it down with milk.

After Lisa, he should have known better. Another model, for cripe's sake! He should've *known* better!

To think he'd almost convinced himself that this one was different. He could have sworn that any woman who could cook pork chops and corn bread, collards and sweet potatoes the way she could—any woman who professed to like gardening, even if she wasn't much good at it—had to be more than just another pretty face.

He should've known better, Gus thought bitterly as he scraped the last few grains of wet sugar from the bottom of his bowl.

So. He would say what he had to say to her, and then he would head for the hills. He sure as hell wasn't going to hang around where he wasn't welcome.

But first he was going to ram home a few words of wisdom.

Wisdom? Like what?

Like, I almost made a mistake, Mariah?

Like, I almost thought we had something going for us. Thought I could fit into your life and you could fit into mine, and together, we might even make us a few little Jessies of our own?

Yeah. Right. As if any woman who moved in the glitzy world all models seemed to prefer would be interested in giving it all up to settle down in a cabin in the mountains with a red-neck carpenter who, for the past couple of decades, had made a fine art of avoiding commitment.

Gus washed his dishes and left them in the drainer. The bathroom was empty, so he showered quickly, packed his toothbrush, then gathered up the rest of his gear and crammed it into his duffel bag. He'd never been one for long goodbyes. Say what needed saying and hit the road, that was his motto.

From the room down the hall he could hear Jessie's chortling, which meant Mariah was getting her dressed, which usually included a fair amount of nose and neck tickling and some belly nuzzling.

He was going to miss that young'un. Miss her real bad. Miss her almost as much as he was going to miss her Aunt Ri.

Hell, he was even going to miss Muddy Landing.

The phone rang and Mariah yelled out and asked him to get it. Gus figured it was the sheriff's office, wanting one of them to come down and give a statement. They'd both done enough talking last night, but to be official, maybe it needed to be done in an official setting.

"Brady residence," he growled.

Hesitation. And then, "Who's this?" an unfamiliar masculine voice demanded.

"Who wants to know?" Gus was in no mood to play guessing games.

"This is Basil Brady. I was calling Mariah. Is she, uh, is she around?"

At 6:27 a.m.? Where the hell else would she be?

Gus could hear unspoken questions sizzling like a live wire. Good. Let the bastard twist in the wind for a few minutes. He deserved it for taking his sister away from her work and dumping his problems into her lap without even asking if it was convenient.

Even though the problem had turned out to be Jessie, who was worth any amount of inconvenience. "She's getting Jessie dressed. Hang on, I'll call her."

While Mariah talked to her brother, Gus took his gear out to the truck. She was still talking when he came back inside, and so he borrowed her tape measure—a tape measure, for crying out loud! In a toolbox!

He measured the place where a dryer would go, and then measured the space between the kitchen sink and the refrigerator for a dishwasher.

And then he stood in the back doorway and watched as a gentle rain beat down on the marsh grass along the river. The river that was not even a real river, but a creek.

Some things, he thought, were not what they appeared to be. Some were. The trick was in knowing the difference.

"Basil and Myrtiss are coming for Jessie," Mariah said, pausing in the opposite doorway. "They're between Brunswick and Darien, headed this way."

"Patched up all their differences, huh?" He didn't give a sweet damn in hell about Basil and Myrtiss and their marital woes, but if she wanted to draw it out, he'd play along.

"Myrtiss was upset because Basil was spending too much time working and not enough with her and the baby, and she needed more help but didn't know how to get his attention."

Gus closed the back door and leaned against it. "Evidently she found a way."

Mariah shrugged. "They're awfully young. Myrtiss is only twenty-two."

"At twenty-two you were, what? The assistant manager of Shatley's feed and seed? With a houseful of kids, I guess you didn't need any help."

"Myrtiss is different. She was the youngest in her family."

"Right. And you were the eldest." Gus was beginning to get the picture. "I made coffee."

The pot was right there in plain sight.

Her fingers pinched creases in the sash of her robe. "I see you're all packed."

It was Gus's turn to shrug. Why was it he couldn't just come right out and demand a few answers?

Such as whether or not last night had meant more to her than just a great lay.

Such as whether or not she could turn her back on the glamorous kind of life she led as a model and be content as the wife of a small-time building contractor. Because she couldn't have both. He couldn't share her. No way would he be able to handle having every dude on three continents lusting after a picture of his wife in a skimpy bathing suit leaning up against a palm tree.

Showing off clothes for a bunch of ladies—that would be different. But these days models did a lot more than just parade down a runway in some ladies' department store.

Why the devil didn't I keep on going south?

Mariah thought, He's leaving. Anger seeped in to replace the sense of desolation that had settled over her when she'd seen his bed neatly spread, his closet empty, his truck pulled around in front of the house.

It occurred to her that the only reason those two crooks had broken in last night was because Gus had moved both vehicles around back, out from under the dripping pine trees.

Dear Lord, what if she'd been here alone with Jessie!

"Gus, I haven't thanked you yet—"

He came away from the doorframe in one swift, sinuous motion, his mind still on what had happened between them in bed a few hours ago. "Don't. For crying out loud, Mariah, you don't owe me any thanks."

"But if you hadn't been here . . . well, I suppose I could've managed by myself, but I have to admit, you did come in handy."

He nearly strangled. "I *came . . . in handy?*"

Mariah's eyes narrowed. Gus's widened. He was talking about the most fantastic sex he'd had in his entire life. What on earth was *she* talking about?

"Well, at least it's all over now, so we can both forget it."

Gus wanted to shake her until her ears rattled. He was seldom driven to violence—never with a woman.

Before he'd met Mariah, that was. And it wasn't violence he wanted to commit, it was lust.

No, dammit, it was love!

Barely containing his passion, he brushed past her and stalked down the hallway. With a sinking heart, Mariah followed the sound of his footsteps. In those battered Western boots, it was impossible not to. She heard Jessie's warbled welcome. "Dus, Dus!" Jessie's limited vocabulary had originally consisted of Mama, Daddy, Ri, no-no and doggy.

Now it included Dus.

Oh, Lord. Now everything was going to include Gus. Everything was going to remind her of him, and she didn't know how she was going to stand it. Having him here had been a mistake. Making love to him had been a real blockbuster of a mistake!

If only she'd been wearing her old gray sweats when she'd run into him instead of that new yellow linen outfit she'd bought at a big discount. If only she'd been wearing her glasses, those plastic-rimmed horrors she had hidden behind practically all her life until, in a fit of rebellion after Vance's defection, she had bought her first pair of contacts.

Then Gus would have seen her the way she really was, and he would never have followed her to Muddy Landing, and after a while she would probably have forgotten all about him.

Of course she would. And chickens would swim.

Dammit, a woman needed to be loved for who she was, not for what she happened to look like! How could a love that was based on looks alone survive gray hair and wrinkles, jowls and veins and liver spots?

The trouble was—and this was something she hadn't dared admit, not even to herself—she was beginning to wonder just who the real Mariah was. Was she the woman who'd been so grateful for a little attention she'd ignored every shred of common sense she possessed?

Or was she Vic's creation? The creation he'd polished up and put on display for nearly a year?

Which one was she? Neither? Both?

Gus lifted Jessie out of her crib. He held her for a long time while she tugged at his beard and played with his bushy eyebrows. Evidently, whatever had ailed her no longer did. "Come on, possum, time to say goodbye," he whispered.

Mariah was waiting in the kitchen. She took the baby from his arms, plopped her in the high chair and handed her a cracker.

Then she turned to Gus. "I don't suppose you'll call and let me know you got home safely," she said, as though it was a foregone conclusion.

"Do you want me to?"

"To call?" She shrugged. "It's up to you. Don't bother if you'd rather not."

They were both dancing all around the subject foremost on their minds. They both knew it. Gus reached for her just as she bent to retrieve the cracker Jessie had thrown on the floor. His arms fell back to his sides. "Sure. I'll give you a call. If you're going to be here."

"Where else would I be?"

"No telling," he said, and tried to make it sound as if the answer wasn't vitally important. "So, look...I'd better be shoving off, but if you ever need anything... That is, if you find out..." How the hell did a guy tell his lady that if she found herself pregnant— or even wanting to be—he'd burn up the highway getting back to her? "Mariah, if you ever need—"

"You already said that."

"Oh. Yeah, I guess I did. Well, look, take care of Jessie, and tell Basil and Myrtiss I'm sorry I couldn't hang around—but not very." His grin was more of a grimace, but at least he made the effort.

"I will. And, Gus, thank you again. For Florida, for the shed and the steps and the plumbing. For last night." She closed her eyes and groaned. "You know what I mean," she muttered.

"Yeah, I know what you mean."

He left before he could make a fool of himself bigtime, but not before he'd hauled her into his arms so close he could count the lashes on her startled eyes just before they swept down, count the freckles on her nose. She had three. And count the ways she had changed his life forever.

Fifty-odd years from now, he might even be able to forgive her for that.

Ten

Well... that's life, kiddo. Shoulders drooping, Mariah waved off the last of her visitors, her false smile fading even as she turned to go back inside to begin putting her house in order.

Oh, Lord ha' mercy, this was going to hurt! Before this past week she hadn't spent more than a few hours with Jessie, and even then, not alone. Now it felt as if her own child had just been torn from her arms.

With Gus, it was more like having her beating heart torn right out of her breast. Everywhere she looked there were reminders. The shabby, familiar living room, with all the knickknacks set out of reach of small hands. The kitchen, where Gus had washed while she'd dried and put away, where he'd fed Jessie while she'd cooked their suppers. The bedroom...

It was going to take more than moving a few shrubs to come to terms with what ailed her this time.

The phone rang just as she poured herself another cup of coffee. It was Burdy. "Basil said you were back home for a spell. Look, Ri, I need a small loan."

"Is it really important?" Mariah asked. "I'm sort of strapped at the moment, but if it's important, I can scrape up something." She was planning to cash in her CD, hoping it would last until she found another job.

"The guys are going to Myrtle Beach for spring break. I've saved up almost enough by working extra hours, but I'm still a little short, so could you please, please lend me a hundred, Ri? I promise, I'll pay you back."

Mariah had a drawerful of IOU's from various members of her family. Once they all got established, she was confident they would repay her. It was the meantime that was a problem.

Still, they were her family. She loved them all dearly, and if they depended on her during an emergency it was only because she'd encouraged them to depend on her. What else was family for?

She promised to put a check in the mail the next day. Then, after putting the dishes in to soak—Basil and Myrtiss had been in a hurry to get home, but not too big a hurry to eat lunch—Mariah went around to the shed.

The shed that Gus had spent almost an entire day shoring up so that it wouldn't collapse.

She got out her mattock and shovel and surveyed the possibilities. It didn't seem fair to move the poor azaleas again. She'd moved them the day she had found herself embracing one of Gus's shirts before putting it in the wash.

The rain had stopped temporarily but it was still cloudy, which suited her mood just fine. Grimly, she eyed the sap-dripping pine trees that branched out over her driveway.

By the time Gus crossed into North Carolina again just south of Charlotte, the rain had all but stopped. A streak of lemony sunlight sliced through slate gray clouds, highlighting a patch of luminous yellow forsythia planted beside an overpass.

He wasn't ready for spring. At the rate he was going, he might never be ready for spring. He was tired from a lack of sleep and from—

Well, what the hell? He was tired, period.

At any rate, he drove on through, knowing that stopping would be a waste of time. He wouldn't be able to sleep. He'd spent the entire trip so far trying to convince himself that he'd had a lucky escape—that men who reached the advanced age of thirty-nine-and-a-half without marrying were obviously not cut out to be husbands.

Unfortunately, he was finding it harder and harder to convince himself.

There were still traces of gray snow banked up against the rocks in his yard. The small A-frame looked cold and empty and unwelcoming. Inside, it was all that and more. He'd forgotten the mess he'd left behind, taking off the way he had after being laid up for a week.

As he went about unpacking his truck and cleaning up his house, he was reminded of Mariah's slap-dash housekeeping. She'd kept things clean, but not exactly tidy. Actually, he'd kind of liked it that way. Even with baby gear crammed in between pieces of furniture that bore mute witness to years of hard living, with her muddy sneakers and his muddy boots beside the door, and a few boxes still waiting to be unpacked, it was a lot more inviting than his place at its neatest.

Hell, except for the basics—a bed, a man-size sofa, a kitchen table for eating, sorting fishing tackle and for the occasional poker game—he'd never even got around to buying furniture.

After putting away several sacks of groceries he'd bought on his way through Marion, he set out a few things for supper. Store-bought sandwiches, store-bought cake, and beer. He ate half a sandwich, drank half a beer and ignored the cake.

Then he snagged a pencil and notepad, dragged a chair up to the telephone and started retrieving his messages. Never one to borrow trouble, he seldom bothered when he was on the road.

Angel had called twice. No news. Just checking up on him. He was to give her a call when he got home from his vacation.

Yeah, right. Some vacation.

His foreman, Pete Davies, had called to say all permits were in hand, and he was headed on down to the coast to get started on the pilings, which would be pumped in by a local crew, which was standard operating procedure.

His dentist had called to remind him of his six-month checkup. That was Angel's doing.

And Kurt called. Gus reached for the bottle and downed the rest of his beer, a grin spreading over his face as he listened to his old buddy telling him that he was finally down from Alaska, out of the coast guard, and looking around for a charter boat with a few good years left in her. And incidentally, he could use a mate if Gus was tired of building houses.

Sweet salvation, Kurt Stryker—*a fisherman?*

Gus thought nostalgically of the old days when he, Kurt and Alex had been known as tall, dark and handsome. Although not necessarily in that order. As a trio, they'd been invincible on the football field, both in high school and later on at N.C. State.

Pretty damned invincible among the cheerleaders, too, come to think of it. Especially Kurt. Fresh off the farm, he'd been so damned handsome he could have been a real pain in the butt, instead of which, he'd turned out to be one of the kindest, most decent men Gus had ever known. He'd been shy, due to a childhood speech problem, but that had made him even more attractive to the women.

The guys had liked him because he was loyal, hardworking, and damned good company. Thanks to years of tossing heavy bales of hay into a wagon, he also happened to have a punishing right cross that came in handy in a brawl.

Good old Kurt, the perennial designated driver.

Gus dialed the number Kurt had given and let it ring a dozen or so times. No message machine. But then, Kurt had never been a gadget freak. Keep it simple and cut your loses, that was the Stryker philosophy. He'd joined the coast guard right out of college, for pretty much the same reason Gus had dropped out just short of graduation. Because they'd both been crazy in love with Dina, the woman Alex had married, who had later divorced him.

Thinking about the past and all the water under the bridge since they'd last been together, Gus hung up the phone, wondering why a man who'd spent all those years flying rescue missions for the U.S.C.G. in Alaska would end up buying a charter boat on the East Coast. Something didn't square up here...

Five nights later in the middle of a poker game with a few members of his building crew who'd be headed down to the coast the next day, Gus threw down his cards, pushed his chips to the center of the table and stood. "I'm outta here, guys. Finish the game, help yourselves to whatever's in the fridge and lock up when you leave, okay?"

"Hey, it's only Thursday, man. We can't get started until the pilings are all in. That'll be Monday, earliest. What's the big rush?"

"No big rush. I'll meet you on the site at seven Monday morning. You've got your instructions. You know where we'll be staying. If I'm a day or so late, go ahead and start without me. Pete's got all the paperwork and the building accounts are all set up."

It was long after midnight when Gus reached Durham. Angel's old house now served as an office for her landscaping business, but Gus still had a key. He let himself in, tossed his gear in a corner and headed for the bed that was still made up in his old room.

The next morning he had just finished loading his pickup when Angel pulled into the parking lot. "Gus! Why didn't you let me know you were... What the dickens are you doing, anyway? Good Lord, don't tell me you finally decided to landscape the mountainside around that crazy tent of yours!"

"That tent, as you call it, happens to be a flaw-lessly designed, flawlessly constructed, supremely efficient—"

"Yeah, yeah, it's the Taj Mahal. Now come here and give me a hug."

"I'm not sure I can reach around you. Sure you didn't swallow a watermelon?"

Proudly, Angel smoothed her green coveralls down over her protruding belly. "Kindly show a little more respect for your nephew, Wydowski."

After dusting off his hands, Gus enveloped sister and nephew together in a gentle bear hug. "You're looking great, honey. Alex must be walking on air these days. By the way, what grows in a soggy, wet-land area of east central Georgia? I picked out a few things, but—"

"A *few* things! You've wiped out my entire spring stock!"

"What, these runts? They'd never have sold, any-way. I picked out the scrawniest stuff I could find, and by the way, I made a list of everything I took. It's on your desk along with a blank check. Just let me know how much so I can square it with the bank, okay?"

Angel rolled her eyes. "If you keep your business accounts the same way you keep your personal accounts, it's a wonder you aren't bankrupt by now."

"Hey, just because you've got a cash register for a heart, that doesn't mean everybody lives by the bottom line. Some of us set our sights on higher things."

Angel leaned against the tank-size luxury sedan Alex had insisted on buying her, telling her he didn't want her rattling around in her old van anymore. "By 'higher things,' I take it you mean long-legged women, Mexican beer, anything sweet, and that fancy 4×4 pickup truck of yours. Gus, why've you trimmed your beard and cut your hair? Unless I'm very much mistaken, that's a new pair of khakis you're wearing, too, and—oh, my, you've even polished your cowboy boots!"

"They're not cowboy boots, they're—"

"Trust me, they're cowboy boots." She narrowed her eyes, which were one shade darker than his own. "Gus, what are you up to?"

"Jeez, can't a guy get a haircut without—"

"I know you, remember? It's a new woman, isn't it? And this one's special, because you didn't trim your beard for Lisa. In fact you've hardly trimmed the thing ever since you grew it right after Dina and Alex—"

"Oh, for crying out loud, would you just get off my back? I happen to be doing a favor for a friend, all right?"

"A woman friend." It was a statement, not a question.

"So?"

"Gus, I'm your only living relative, not counting Ashfield, here, so would you please just tell me what's going on?"

"Ashfield!"

"It happens to be a family name on Alex's mother's side. Don't change the subject. Now, who is she and why didn't you just go to a florist and buy her a few dozen roses instead of raiding my spring stock? The kind of women you collect wouldn't know a ficus from a fiddlehead fern." Looking suddenly worried, Angel placed a small, square hand on Gus's arm. "Gus, is this serious, or is it some kind of a practical joke?"

Gus shook his head in resignation. "Put away the thumbscrews. I give up. You're right, it's a woman, and I think maybe it might be serious. On my part, at least. And yeah, I know I'm asking for trouble but I'm going after her anyway, so you might as well wish me luck."

Myrtiss called from Atlanta late on the night they got home. Mariah nearly broke her neck getting to the phone, and then had to force down the surge of disappointment when she heard her sister-in-law's voice.

"Is Jessie all right?"

"She's in bed, and yes, she's just fine, but Mariah, what on earth is a dus? She keeps asking for a dus-dus."

Mariah made a sound that was somewhere between a laugh and a sob. "She's picking up new words right and left these days, isn't she? By the way, I found a teething ring under the sofa. Shall I mail it, or does she have spares?''

"Just trash it, I've got half a dozen, at least. Mariah, I didn't thank you properly. I wanted to explain, but not with Basil there.''

"You don't have to explain, I think I understand.''

"Do you, really? Did you know that I was always sort of intimidated by you?''

"You were?'' Mariah had sometimes suspected her young sister-in-law might resent her, but *intimidate?* She couldn't intimidate her own shadow.

"I mean, you've always been so tall and sure of yourself and everything, and—''

"Tall, I'll admit to. I hire out as a flagpole on holidays. But sure of myself? Honey, you just don't know!''

"Well, Basil always talks about how you worked so hard to see them all through school, looking after them while you were working a full-time job, and all. He's always holding you up as an example, saying Ri does this and Ri does that. I hate to say it, but sometimes I used to wish he'd been an only child.''

"Good gracious, in that case, I don't blame you. That brother of mine has always had a few chips missing when it comes to relating to other people. I think part of the problem is that he was the only boy in a household of females, but more than that, he never had time to play while we were growing up. Now his computers are like a game to him. Lucky for you and Jessie, he's good enough to make a living at it, but you have to remember that in some ways, he's still just a boy, and boys need discipline. The trick is to be firm and consistent and at the same time, make sure he always knows you love him."

"Yes, well . . . first you have to get his attention."

Mariah chuckled. "Oh, I think you managed to do that, all right. It took a lot of courage to go off and leave Jessie with my brother, even knowing he'd scout out a baby-sitter before the first diaper needed changing."

This time it was Myrtiss who laughed. It occurred to Mariah that she sounded not quite so young and resentful as she had only a moment ago. "You know I'd never have dared to leave if I hadn't been pretty sure Basil would call on you for help and you'd manage somehow to be there for him. I knew Jessie would be in good hands. And Mariah, it worked. Basil says he's learned his lesson, and that it didn't take him long to find out that working and looking after a baby single-handed can be a real hassle." She giggled. "I don't know how we're going to manage with the next one. We'll probably have to call on you for help again. Have you considered moving to Atlanta? We have models there, too, you know."

"No, I haven't, and the next *what?*"

"Well, of course nothing's certain yet, but we sort of had a second honeymoon on the way back home. Basil insisted on staying at this place that had a Jacuzzi and these funky beds and all, and . . . well, you how those things are."

Mariah didn't. She would like to, but so far, she hadn't been offered the opportunity. "Steamed up his glasses, huh? Am I to infer that Basil didn't spend all his time playing with his laptop?"

"Ma-*ri*-ah!"

"Computer! I meant his computer!" They both giggled. Hanging up the phone a few minutes later, Mariah told herself it was beginning to look as if her entire future was being mapped out without any input from her.

Move to Atlanta? No way. "Dammit, sooner or later, I'm going to have to wean that mob," she muttered.

That had been Tuesday night. On Wednesday morning, she mailed out a carefully composed résumé to every hardware store she could find listed in Waycross and Brunswick on the off chance that they needed an experienced assistant manager. If she had to go farther afield than that, she'd try Savannah or Athens, not Atlanta.

If worse came to worst, she could always go back to Vic. She had jumped at the chance of a modeling career the first time because it looked so glamorous and exciting. It hadn't taken her long to discover that glamour and excitement were not all they were cracked up to be.

Oh, she could do it if she had to—and it was nice to know she had the option—but she'd much rather muddle along at her own speed, in her own comfortable neck of the woods.

The trouble was, her neck of the woods didn't offer much in the way of a livelihood.

The next morning she cashed in her slightly immature CD, paid the seven-dollar penalty, sent a check to Burdina and had Moe Chitty give her car a thorough going-over, replacing whatever needed replacing, tightening up all the nuts and bolts that driving on bumpy clay roads had loosened.

That afternoon she set her houseplants outside under the eaves, filled all the bird feeders and scattered the last of the sunflower seeds on the ground for the doves and the squirrels to fight over.

By Friday afternoon she was ready to go. Jobless or not, she had earned herself a vacation. It had been so long since she'd had one, she'd almost forgotten how, but maybe if she just set out in the general direction of someplace interesting—the mountains of North Carolina, for instance....

Eleven

———

Mariah got as far as the front door, car keys in her hand. At the sight of the familiar pickup truck pulling up in her driveway, its bed resembling a portable jungle, she started laughing, which made it all the harder to understand why her eyes should be watering.

"What is this, an arbor day parade float?" she called through the screen door. "You're blocking my driveway, Wydowski. What are you doing here, anyway? Did you forget something?"

Gus swung open the door of his truck and climbed out, looking even prouder, tougher, more invincible than she'd remembered.

Not that she hadn't memorized every hair on his head, every line and scar on his wonderful face. An overhead sun glinted down on his brass buckle, his polished boots, and picked out the hint of red in his beard and a few silver strands in his freshly trimmed hair. He looked tanned and fit and altogether beautiful, which, for some reason, brought fresh tears to her eyes.

"I didn't think you were coming back," she said, her eyes brimming with joy and hope and uncertainty as she went to meet him.

"I wasn't. That is, I tried not to. It didn't work."

He sauntered up to stand in front of her, hands shoved into the pockets of his stiff new jeans. Now that he was closer, she thought he didn't look quite so sure of himself.

But she wasn't taking anything for granted. "What didn't work?"

"Me," he said with a self-conscious grin.

"Did you, um, find a job in the area? Building something, I mean?"

"Nope."

"I give up," she said helplessly. "Gus, what's going on? What are all those trees in the back of your truck?"

"Just some stuff I picked up. They're all tagged if you need to know the names." He held out a square, callosed hand, and like a fool, she took it, and then it was too late. He was standing much too close. She could smell the familiar Gus scent of coffee, soap and leather, and he wasn't even wearing his leather coat.

What Gus smelled was lilacs. It was too early for them to be blooming, even if she'd had any. Maybe he'd get her a few. She might like that.

"I like that thing you're wearing." He indicated the creamy yellow slacks and the gauzy matching top that was knotted below her waist. She wore a lot of yellow. On her it looked good.

On her, anything looked good!

She had on those damned clogs again, which put her eyes on a level with his own, and her lips...

Gus groaned. He wrapped his arms around her and buried his face in her hair. "I missed you," he whispered, his voice husky and deep. "God, how I missed you, Mariah."

"You almost did, literally," she replied when she could make her voice work again. "I was actually on my way out the door. See? Here are my car keys." She jangled them beside his left ear. "I was planning to drive north and maybe explore the area around Banner Elk, only I'm not quite sure where it is."

Gus chuckled, and then he threw back his head and roared. "You're kidding, right? You were actually coming after *me?*"

She stiffened in his arms. "Well, you don't have to take it personally. You're not the only attraction the mountains have to offer."

"Ski season's over, honey," he reminded her gently.

"I don't ski."

"Well, there's trout fishing, but—"

"I don't have a trout pole."

Gus's arms tightened. He closed his eyes and wondered what he would have done if he'd arrived and she'd been gone. Planted a truckload of shrubbery while he waited, probably. Dug up a forest or two.

"Let's go inside," he said gruffly. "We need to talk first."

"First before what?"

Swinging her around toward the house, Gus walked beside her, one arm around her waist. "What do you think?"

"Before we start planting all that stuff in your truck? Gus, if you meant that for me, I think it's only fair to tell you that I'm thinking about putting the house on the market. For sale this time, not for rent."

They passed under the pine trees and Gus eyed the bare roots of a twenty-foot specimen. She had a system all her own that consisted of undermining the roots with a mattock, cutting them off underground, and then toppling the entire tree. It was easier, she'd said, to find someone to cut up and haul off a load of firewood than it was to find someone to grub up a stump.

Looking at her now, with that cloud of weimaraner-colored hair, those cheek bones—those legs—he thought, Sweet salvation, was there ever such a woman?

"A little landscaping might help it sell."

"For a fish camp? That's all it's good for. Nobody ever moves to Muddy Landing to live anymore. We're all moving away to find work."

"So maybe we'll keep it as a vacation place, how's that?" He tried to sound calm and thoughtful, just as if he weren't so nervous his palms were sweating.

Just as if proposing to a woman was no big deal.

Just as if he weren't already randy as a goat, just seeing her, touching her. It was a wonder she hadn't noticed. There was a lot to be said for baggy khakis.

So far, he hadn't dared to kiss her, because if he kissed her before they got inside the house, he might wind up laying her on the ground and taking her right there, which was no way to treat a lady.

Besides, he liked that yellow outfit she was wearing too much to risk it on a muddy driveway. She'd been wearing yellow the first time he'd seen her. Yellow splashed with red, and smelling of lilacs and rain and cherry flavoring.

He barely made it through the door. "We've got to talk," he said, trying to look serious instead of lecherous.

It didn't work. With a groan, he gathered her in his arms and took her with a kiss that rocked him right down to his boot heels. Before he'd even begun to slake his thirst, he knew it wasn't going to be enough— not nearly enough.

"Take off those damned shoes," he muttered.

"I can talk with my shoes on."

Bumping toes and knees, he began backing her along the hallway toward the bedroom. "You can talk without 'em, too. You can talk even better without your clothes on." And he kissed her again.

"Gus, what are you—"

He lifted his face, his eyes pleading. "Mariah, you see before you a desperate man. I've got a limited amount of time—"

Her heart sank at that revelation.

"And a limited amount of patience. Think of a big stick of dynamite on a very short fuse."

She knew about short fuses. He was sizzling all the way down to the quick already.

"Woman, if you don't want me in your bed, you'd better speak up real fast."

She wanted him in her bed. That was the trouble. She wanted him permanently, temporarily—wanted him any way she could have him, for as long as she could manage to keep him.

"How much time?" she asked.

"Enough."

"You'd better be telling me the truth." Stepping out of her clogs, she indicated his boots. "No fair. If I'm going to be barefooted, then you are, too."

"Honey, that's not all that's going to be bare." Gus hopped on first one foot and then the other, shucking off his boots and his brand new socks. His hands went to the flat knot at the waist of her cross-over blouse, and he made short work of what had taken her all of five minutes to get right. Next he tackled her slacks, catching the waistband of her yellow panties and sliding them down over her hips.

His gaze moved over her like a laser beam, lingering on the lacy bra that was all she was wearing now that her pants were puddled around her bare feet. "We're going to take this slow and easy," he promised in a husky whisper, and she nodded.

Gus unbuckled his belt and she heard the sound of a zipper. She still hadn't lowered her gaze from his. Didn't dare. Her heart was already pounding so hard it shook her whole body. "But not too slow and easy," she said anxiously.

Lord ha' mercy, he was magnificent! She'd forgotten how lean and flat his waist was, how his sides flared out just under his arms. And those shoulders...

There was probably a name for all those muscles, just as there was probably a name for whatever it was that made her want to hang on to him and never, ever let him go—made her want to taste him and feel him and absorb him into her body until she couldn't tell where she ended and he began.

"I hope you aren't expected anywhere in the near future," Gus said, his hands trembling as he folded back the chenille spread and laid her down on the crisp, cool sheets. "This may take a while."

It took less than three minutes. The first time, at least. One touch and they both went up in flames. Mariah wrapped her legs around his hard, sweat-sleeked body and held on while Gus rode her fiercely, driving them both higher and harder as he felt her begin to spasm around him.

With a guttural groan, he collapsed, still holding her tightly in his arms. "Sweet salvation," he muttered. "I needed that."

Mariah had needed it, too, but she needed far more than one blazing moment of bliss, no matter how earth-shaking it had been. "Gus, do you think..." She paused, uncertain how to say what she needed to say.

"On rare occasions." He lifted his head to smile down at her, his face still flushed, his breathing deep and harsh. "I'm sorry, sweetheart, I promised myself

I'd take things one step at a time—give you a chance to get used to the idea."

She was almost afraid to ask. "What idea?"

"The idea of me. Sort of, uh, permanently?" He ventured one swift, unreadable look, then lowered his head to the pillow beside her. "I'm pretty adaptable. I mean, if you want to go back to modeling, I guess I could handle that as long as—"

"No."

He lifted his head again, and Mariah thought it was as if a light had gone out behind his eyes. "No?"

"I mean, Gus, I can't breathe. Could you move just a little bit?"

Gathering her in his arms, Gus deftly rearranged their relative positions until he was flat on his back, with Mariah sprawled on top of him. "There, that better?"

"Not much. At least not when it comes to trying to think clearly."

His laughter was slow in coming, and when it did, it set off all sorts of repercussions in the most sensitive areas of her body. "Never let it be said that I'm not an equal opportunity lover."

"Gus!" Mariah felt a rush of heat sting her cheeks. If she'd been ten years younger, she might have thought she was blushing. She was propped up on her elbows, but with a minimum of effort Gus managed to bring her face down to his level. The kiss involved a lot of exploration on both sides, gentle at first, then fierce and openly carnal.

This time, they really did take it slow and easy, savoring every touch, every taste—the discovery of every exquisite, quicksilver nerve ending. Pausing for breath, Gus closed his eyes and groaned. When he opened them again, it was to gaze up at the woman sitting so proud and tall astride his body, her long sleek legs caressing his flanks with every subtle movement of her hips.

"You're killing me by slow, sweet degrees," he grated.

"I can't help it, I love this feeling of power."

"Keep it up and you'll be a widow before you're even a wife." He gripped her shoulders and held her still while he thrust higher, harder, driving them over the edge in a blind explosion of sheer sensation. His last lucid thought as he lapsed into semiconsciousness was that she hadn't yet said she would.

Later, as they lay propped up in bed sipping coffee—it was strong and dark and sweet, just the way Gus liked it—he reminded her that she had not yet given him an answer.

"I didn't? Which question didn't I answer? I thought we'd covered everything. I told you, didn't I, that Jessie's still asking for Dus-Dus?"

At that, he beamed. "Hey, I was pretty good, wasn't I?"

"You mean, as a baby-sitter?"

"Well, I haven't had a whole lot of practice, but I wasn't half bad."

"Oh. I thought you meant as a lover," she teased gently.

Gus's arm tightened around her and her head found the place on his shoulder that pillowed it so perfectly. "Like I said, with a little more practice..."

"I thought you had a problem with time?" Mariah ventured.

"Nothing we can't work out. How do you feel about a working honeymoon at the beach?"

"I don't even have a job."

His hand moved under the covers and found a place in the crease of her thigh where she'd just discovered she was incredibly sensitive. "I'm offering you one," he said gruffly.

Mariah was beyond playing games. "Gus, have you really thought about it? I mean, I know you don't have a lot of use for models, not that—"

"I can adapt."

"Not that I want to go on modeling. I'd rather find something a lot less visible—maybe something out-doors."

"Like I said, I'm easy. I can support us both, but if you'd rather work until the babies start coming, I can handle that, too."

The babies. Oh, good gracious! "But what if we're not compatible? You really haven't known me all that long."

"Okay, what about a deal, then?" He carefully placed his cup on the bedside table, took hers and placed it beside his, then gathered up both her hands in both of his. "We've already wasted a lot of time, so what do you say we get married right away, I'll find us a place of our own instead of sharing with the guys, and we'll see how you like the coast? After that, we can spend some time in the mountains, and in a year or so, maybe build something of our own somewhere in between—something big enough to hold a family. I mean, in case Jessie wants to come for a visit. What do you think?''

Mariah felt like pinching herself. She couldn't believe it was actually happening. ''You haven't said anything at all about love.''

''Yeah, well . . . I guess it's not one of those things a guy talks about. I did ask you to marry me, didn't I? I've never done that before. Came close a couple of times, but I never felt like this. Nowhere near it.''

''Does that mean you do?''

''What, love you? Yeah.'' He stared down at their joined hands, and then he sighed. ''Yeah, I do. I mean, big-time. As in, I can't imagine the rest of my life unless you're a great big part of it. That kind of love.''

Mariah nodded thoughtfully. ''Hmm. In that case, I reckon we could give it a try. All right then,'' she said decisively. ''I'll marry you, and we'll go wherever you need to go, and maybe over the next fifty years or so we can work out the details.''

''Lady, you've got yourself one great big deal. Shake on it!'' His slate blue eyes darkened even as they began to glow.

Smiling in a way that made the Mona Lisa seem like a stand-up comic, Mariah whispered, ''I've got a much better idea.''

And she had.

*   *   *   *   *

COMING NEXT MONTH

It's Silhouette Desire's 1000th birthday! Join us for a spectacular three-month celebration, starring your favorite authors and the hottest heroes of the decade!

#991 SADDLE UP—Mary Lynn Baxter

One night with Bridget Martin had cost April's *Man of the Month*, single dad Jeremiah Davis, his bachelorhood! But would his new bride be the perfect mom for his little girl?

#992 THE GROOM, I PRESUME?—Annette Broadrick
Daughters of Texas

Maribeth O'Brien was everything Chris Cochran wanted in a woman. So when she was left at the altar by her delinquent groom, Chris stepped in and said, "I do"!

#993 FATHER OF THE BRAT—Elizabeth Bevarly
From Here to Paternity

Maddy Garrett had never liked arrogant Carver Venner. But now he needed her help—and Maddy couldn't resist his adorable daughter...or the sexy single dad!

#994 A STRANGER IN TEXAS—Lass Small

One passionate encounter with a handsome stranger had left Jessica Channing one very pregnant woman. Now the mysterious man was back, determined to discover Jessica's secret!

#995 FORGOTTEN VOWS—Modean Moon
The Wedding Night

Although Edward Carlton claimed his lovely bride had left him on their wedding night, Jennie didn't remember her husband. But she'd do anything to discover the truth about her past—and her marriage....

#996 TWO WEDDINGS AND A BRIDE—Anne Eames
Debut Author

Brand-new bride Catherine Mason was furious when she caught her groom kissing her bridesmaid! So she went on her honeymoon with handsome Jake Alley—and hoped another wedding would soon be on the way....

MILLION DOLLAR SWEEPSTAKES

SWP-M96

THE PROTECTORS

by Beverly Barton

Trained to protect, ready to lay their lives on the line, but unprepared for the power of love.

Award-winning author Beverly Barton brings you
Ashe McLaughlin, Sam Dundee and J. T. Blackwood...
three rugged, sexy ex-government agents—each with a
special woman to protect.

J.T. Blackwood is six feet four inches of whipcord-lean man.
And in April, in BLACKWOOD'S WOMAN (IM #707), the
former secret service agent returns to his New Mexico ranch
for a well-deserved vacation, and finds his most dangerous
assignment yet—Joanna Beaumont. The terror Joanna fled
from five years ago has suddenly found her. Now only J.T.
stands between his beautiful tenant's deadly past and her
future...a future he is determined to share with her.

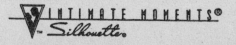

INTIMATE MOMENTS®
Silhouette®

BBPROT3

SILHOUETTE®

Desire®

Presents the conclusion of

SONS AND *Lovers*

COMING IN MARCH 1996

RIDGE: THE AVENGER by Leanne Banks

It was bad enough Ridge Jackson had been hired to protect
feisty Dara Seabrook, now he was finding it impossible to
resist the one woman who could never be his!

"For the best mini-series of the decade, tune into
SONS AND LOVERS, a magnificent trilogy created
by three of romance's most gifted talents."

—Harriet Klausner
Affaire de Coeur

Also Available:

SD #975 LUCAS: THE LONER—Cindy Gerard (1/96)
SD # 981 REESE: THE UNTAMED—Susan Connell (2/96)

As seen on TV!
Free Gift Offer

With a Free Gift proof-of-purchase from any Silhouette® book,
you can receive a beautiful cubic zirconia pendant.

This gorgeous marquise-shaped stone is a genuine cubic
zirconia—accented by an 18" gold tone necklace.

(Approximate retail value $19.95)

Send for yours today...
compliments of ▼ *Silhouette*®

To receive your free gift, a cubic zirconia pendant, send us one original proof-of-
purchase, photocopies not accepted, from the back of any Silhouette Romance™,
Silhouette Desire®, Silhouette Special Edition®, Silhouette Intimate Moments®
or Silhouette Shadows™ title available in February, March or April at your favorite
retail outlet, together with the Free Gift Certificate, plus a check or money order for
$1.75 U.S./$2.25 CAN. (do not send cash) to cover postage and handling, payable
to Silhouette Free Gift Offer. We will send you the specified gift. Allow 6 to 8 weeks for
delivery. Offer good until April 30, 1996 or while quantities last. Offer valid in the U.S. and
Canada only.

Free Gift Certificate

Name: _____

Address: _____

City: _____ State/Province: _____ Zip/Postal Code: _____

Mail this certificate, one proof-of-purchase and a check or money order for postage
and handling to: SILHOUETTE FREE GIFT OFFER 1996. In the U.S.: 3010 Walden
Avenue, P.O. Box 9057, Buffalo NY 14269-9057. In Canada: P.O. Box 622, Fort Erie,

---

FREE GIFT OFFER
ONE PROOF-OF-PURCHASE

079-KBZ-R

To collect your fabulous FREE GIFT, a cubic zirconia pendant, you must include this
original proof-of-purchase for each gift with the properly completed Free Gift Certificate.

079-KBZ-R

It's time you joined…

THE BABY OF THE MONTH CLUB

Silhouette Desire proudly presents *Husband: Optional*, book four of RITA Award-winning author Marie Ferrarella's miniseries, THE BABY OF THE MONTH CLUB, coming your way in March 1996.

She wasn't fooling him. Jackson Cain knew the baby Mallory Flannigan had borne was his…no matter that she *claimed* a conveniently absentee lover was Joshua's true dad. And though Jackson had left her once to "find" his true feelings, nothing was going to keep him away from this ready-made family now….

Do You Take This Child? We certainly hope you do, because in April 1996 Silhouette Romance will feature this final book in Marie Ferrarella's wonderful miniseries, THE BABY OF THE MONTH CLUB, found only in— *Silhouette*®

You're About to Become a

Become a

Privileged

Woman

**Reap the rewards of fabulous free gifts and
benefits with proofs-of-purchase from
Silhouette and Harlequin books**

Pages & Privileges™

**It's our way of thanking you for
buying our books at your
favorite retail stores.**

```
┌──────────────────────┐
│ 📖 PROOF OF  SD-PP115 │
│    PURCHASE           │
│ Offer expires October 31, 1996 │
└──────────────────────┘
```

**Harlequin and Silhouette—
the most privileged readers in the world!**

**For more information about Harlequin and
Silhouette's PAGES & PRIVILEGES program call the
Pages & Privileges Benefits Desk: 1-503-794-2499**

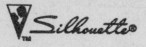

SD-PP115